# Lost Freedom

Madyson Ann Evans

Anishinaabeque Publishing—Baraga, MI
Paperback ISBN: 979-8-218-91417-2
eBook ISBN: 979-8-2955-6819-0
Library of Congress Control Number: 2026901796
Title: *Lost Freedom*
Author: Madyson Ann Evans
Digital distribution | 2026
Paperback | 2026

This is a work of fiction. The characters, names, incidents, places, and dialogue are products of the author's imagination, and are not to be construed as real.

Published in the United States by New Book Authors Publishing

# Dedication

To my mom and dad, my family, friends, and my teachers. Thank you for being the light in this journey. I appreciate all of you.

# Chapter One

### Safety

*Children.*
*Lost and alone.*
*Locked inside of a prison,*
*unable to go back home.*
*Trapped in a Tombstone,*
*full of the weary,*
*and the bodies of the rest,*
*who were left for the dead.*

The safe room was quiet, the only noise being the giggle of one of the youngest children. Her voice bouncing from the bright white walls that seemed to reflect off the light above their heads, like the glow of the sun, even though sunlight was no longer in their grasp.

Charlie sat in the corner silently, watching as the other kids played and danced. Luck was on their side with the giant safe room, more of a skill. Millie had picked it quickly since she knew her way around the lab at the time.

Their savior stood in the kitchen, taking an apple out of the wooden fruit bowl that she had refilled that morning. Charlie forced her eyes away since staring was rude.

"Hey Charlie! Do you want one?" Millie called over. She looked up and watched the girl toss the apple. She caught the red vibrant fruit and snuggled it into her fingers.

"Thank you," muttered the young girl, cupping the apple in her hands and taking a bite.

Millie stayed in the kitchen, and Charlie guessed she was looking for something to eat for everybody, since none of them had eaten lunch yet. Food hadn't been made at dinner, breakfast, or lunch in months, only grabbed from the fridge or given.

Time had been lost, every day had been quick and swift. Every hour had been the same, sleeping, eating, sometimes playing, and then sleeping again. All of it was the same, every hour, every minute, every second, all of it. No difference.

Sally ran around, dodging Mitchell in his attempts to tag her in their game. Charlie continued eating the apple, finally having something to do besides playing tag. That's the only game they ever played that was worth their time, besides the brutal and terrifying stories Mitchell and Sally roleplayed. The place was big but wasn't that large for hide and seek. Everyone knew the hiding spots on day three of being trapped. There wasn't a point in trying to act like you were having fun by finding someone in the same anticipated spots repeatedly.

She heard a door opening down the hallway she was sitting next to, so she leaned her head over to look through it. Lisa was walking down from her bedroom. She looked brand new, unlike her exhausted appearance from before. Her replenished brown sparkly eyes crossed over to Charlie, glistening in the light.

Charlie smiled awkwardly, going back into her curled up sitting position. Michael was still by the door, trying his best to get it unlocked. No one believed in him; they wanted to, but everyone had lost hope at that point, and had no faith left in believing, besides Millie.

Millie looked over at Lisa, giving her a warm smile. "Are you hungry?" She opened the tiny refrigerator.

"No, I'm alright," she declined, drawing her attention to her brother, trying to open the door still. He had been doing this for years probably, barely eating or sleeping. He had just been so determined, so desperate to open that door that had locked them inside the room for however long it had been.

"You think he will get it open someday?" Lisa wondered, saying her thoughts out loud.

Charlie looked over at Michael while she pondered about it, maybe one day he might, but that thought felt so wrong. It wasn't going to happen, she knew it.

"Hopefully." That was all Charlie said.

Sally slowed her pace once she whipped around over at Millie who was holding another delicious snack for her.

The girl didn't hesitate when she spotted it, running over and taking the apple, whispering thank you and sprinting off with it in her hand. Millie smiled with a small piece of happiness inside of her heart, one of the others that felt joy in this place. Happiness meant hope, faith, something Charlie would probably never have again. Millie continued to look for something for herself. Mitchell looked over at a chair and sat down, his legs aching from chasing Sally around the main room all morning. A wish occurred to him out of some place he didn't know of. Some natural light would feel great, or maybe windows. It felt like they hadn't been outside in years, almost a decade at least; they probably hadn't, but he couldn't tell; none of them could.

The room they had been locked in was cozy, filled with a living room, kitchen, and bedrooms enough for all of them. It felt like home occasionally, a regular home they all missed dearly.

A bathroom was also included, along with enough toilet paper for a long time, a lot of food, all of it being canned. The cold food had spoiled after a week of being in the room, before time had run away from the kids. Someone must have restocked it a day or so before the attack.

There was a long storage closet for whatever, mostly the toilet paper and canned food, a broom and some mops for cleaning and keeping things spotless. Millie usually did it, and some others offered help.

Michael fidgeted inside of a hole he and Millie had cut out in the large hollow door. His hand reached inside, feeling nothing but wires and gears.

"Be careful, Michael. No one wants you to get electrocuted," Millie warned, sliding out of the kitchen. Michael didn't say anything, still snooping about in the dark.

"Michael," Millie said, her voice switching into a stern, and cold demeanor, a motherly instinct taking control. Because of course it did.

Michael whipped his head around, showing her that she had his attention.

"I know," he assured with a cocky smile, going back to looking around in the electric powered door.

She sighed, turning her attention back to Charlie, who was still sitting on the ground. Alone, sad, tired, all of it, physically and emotionally. Deep inside, everyone felt the same way.


Charlie watched as Millie sat down next to her with the bible she always carried around clutched in her arms, finally being able to rest after the long morning of helping everyone.

The scars all over her body stood out from most of her features. She had been fighting back during the attack, and had been given a reminder of it, but the mark on her hand always caught her eye.

*Experiment One.*

Charlie remembered that the Experiments numbers were ordered to how strong they would be, depending on the powers they were 'gifted,' but she didn't want to recall that, because it made her think some horrible thought of superiority would infect her, and she didn't believe that.

"Is it the scars?" Millie noticed her staring, looking up from the book with an amused expression.

"Yeah," Charlie said. "What did…cause that day?"

She hadn't fully seen it, since Millie had pushed her back before she had the chance to. Her friend hesitated to speak about it, before finally answering.

"A monster." Those two words didn't give much context, but that was the most she had gotten, after asking the very same question for the tenth time.

"Did…you kill it?"

Millie turned her eyes to her again, they looked very sincere that time.

"No. I was only able to knock it down. Best I could do."

"Wouldn't have it been better to just kill it when you had the chance?" Why was she asking so many questions?

"I couldn't do so." Millie kept her smile, but it was close to fading.

*It's good to be merciful, but personally in some moments…brutality is needed*, the words that Millie had said once appeared in her mind. Though they didn't match the situation, they simply arrived.

Charlie glared at the inedible part of the apple; her attention was soon drawn to the trash can in the clear range of a shot.

Scooching herself upward, she prepared to throw it. Millie watched as the now small fruit flew past her, landing directly into the trash can, it wobbled for a couple seconds, then ended with a thud. Charlie looked out at the children as she slowly rested her back against the wall once again, wishing the material wasn't immune to her powers as well. Maybe she could've unlocked the door by now, or whatever was keeping them caged. Millie opened her book and started reading, Charlie remembered that Millie had already finished the entire book. She was just looking over some verses or words.

Her head hurt to the point where she had to rest against the cold foam like material behind her; her eyes were barely capable of opening; Millie noticed her weariness.

"Maybe you should go to bed, if you are that tired," she suggested, starting to get up from her imaginary comfortable seat once she shut the book loudly, sending an echo throughout the room.

Charlie thought about it for a moment; she thought hard as if it was some sort of math problem they had given her a while back. She eventually made up her mind, getting up from the floor as well, "Yeah, I guess I will."

A yawn escaped her throat, as she turned down the hall next to her while stretching her arms into the air. She heard the muffled voices of the kids as she stumbled further away. Her steps were slow and working hard like she had been running for hours. She had only been sitting, but Charlie guessed her bum was a little sore after that.

She soon reached the tall wooden door, at least for her it was. She gripped the doorknob, twisting it quickly and using it as a hold for her body as she walked in. Charlie strode over to her bed, falling back and collapsing, curling up into a ball as she fell directly into the purple blanket. It was cold, it felt nice since she was overwhelmed by sweat. When were they going to get out of here? She wanted it to happen; she wanted everything to change, to try and shield them all from the tragedies in their lives, including herself. She wanted to be free. Charlie rolled over to face the ceiling.

The girl felt the tears rolling down her face when thinking about it, along with the sad feeling of imprisonment. She just wished they could be free, free from this dungeon, free from the torment that haunted herself and others. With little freedom in a small apartment sized room, she was surprised they hadn't gone insane yet. Her hand lay beside her; she watched as her fingers trembled for little to no reason, probably because of her tears. She cried silently, unable to notice Millie standing in the ajar door.

"Are you OKAY, Charlie?" Her voice was soft, unlike before.

"Yeah, I'm fine, can I just be alone?"

"Are you sure?" Mother Millie, as always.

"Please." Not an answer to her question, more like a plea.

There was a quiet pause before the door moved a little, hesitation from Millie who was about to close it.

"As you wish. Try and sleep, okay?"

The door finally closed, and the room was surrounded in darkness, and a silent atmosphere, peaceful, but it wasn't enough to comfort her.

Nothing felt like it was enough anymore, yet they were everything.

# Chapter Two
### Closer to the Door of Freedom

Charlie hadn't realized she had cried to herself the whole entire day. Millie had respected her wishes of being left alone but had checked in on her to ask her if she was hungry. Charlie had refused and hadn't realized that dinner must have been commencing. When she had left, everyone was waiting at the bathroom door, preparing for bed. She joined them, having a chat with Lisa. She hadn't slept at all, only crying to herself and praying for sleep to come and take her, to put her into some sort of dream that would cover up the despair. Even a second would have made her feel a sliver of joy; just a second of freedom would fill her with peace.

The last time the outside world was in her view, was when she was with her mother, before her entire life was batted into chaos. The girl knew it was the same type of situation from others' points of view but told in a different story. At least once, some pictures would help, just to see some other person, some other form of life. It's not like she hated the people she lived with now; the girl just wanted to see another child or adult, just one time, just once.

Once everyone was done, the place went silent, pure silence. The only sound being Michael's annoying and disruptive snoring, by now she thought she would get used to it. Charlie was sure others felt the same way. Poor Lisa.

Sally tossed and turned in her small bed, plugging her ears in hopes it would help. She eventually curved the pillow over her ears, groaning with the annoyance of the kid sleeping in the other room. Soon, sleep whisked her away, into a dream far worse.

Charlie crushed the pillow over her ears, rolling over onto her stomach and clenching her teeth in anger. It didn't help; nothing did. She had tried everything, a sleeping mask, music from her almost dead radio, but nothing was working. All of it was now plopped beside her bed.

The night was cold, cold like usual. She had heard a long time ago that the heat was damaged in this safe room; others didn't know how she remembered that when she mentioned it. She breathed out a cold fog from her mouth every time she even breathed.

Charlie wished she could see the sky, the stars, and the moon, but the only sky she saw was the pale brown roof over her head; she wondered if it would all come tumbling down on her one day. Charlie lay on her back, spreading her arms out until one of them left the safety of the bed. She had heard stories of 'monsters being under the bed' when she was younger, but she didn't care anymore, since getting trapped in the safe room was horror by itself. Herself and others were tossed into a nightmare, something that would never let them wake up, escape from it. She wasn't sure if there was an escape. There hadn't been one for however long that door had shut on them. Usually in those situations the door was able to be opened, but the engineers or whoever designed this place thought it was a good idea to make the door lock from the outside. The safe room they were stuck in wasn't used on top of that and hadn't been tended to often. So, when that door had shut, it had immediately locked, keeping them inside of a cozy cell for possibly a year or more.

The white pajamas were soft, the only other thing the group could wear besides their white gowns which had to be washed at eleven every night, so they could be ready in the morning, and the group could swap them out. Charlie heard the rumble of the washing machine in her ears; someone would get up every night and put the gowns into the drying machine next, mostly Millie. Charlie sat there for a while, realizing no one was going to get up. So, she sighed and untucked the blanket from her body.

The girl wobbled to the door, opening it with a loud creak that croaked through the hallway. The halls were always silent. When she was younger, she used to not want to leave her room at night, but why did that matter now? The only thing that triggered her was the loud and obnoxious rumbling coming from Michael's room as she passed it. The corner approached her in her vision. Walking around it, she was relieved to see they had ended right on time. Charlie picked the gowns out of the washing machine one by one, throwing them into the dryer quickly. She wanted to get back to bed as fast as possible.

She plopped down the last of the gowns into the dryer, grabbing a sheet without even looking at it and tossing into the hole. To her annoyance, it floated down right back on the door. Charlie slid it back in.

She heard a small breath of relief behind her; she turned around, only to see Millie leaning on the wall.

"Gosh, that was quick. Did that wake you up?" Millie chuckled as she asked quietly, her dark blue eyes staring at Charlie in the dim illumination of the light above them.

"I didn't hear anyone, so..." Charlie shrugged, her voice dull and bare as she walked past Millie and back to bed.

"Thank you for doing that." Charlie heard the whisper as she reached her destination.

"My pleasure." The words left Charlie's mouth quietly.

"Actually, try to sleep, please. You haven't been fully awake in months," Millie pleaded one last time before Charlie exited her vision through her doorway without an answer.

Millie watched as she closed the door to her room, the hall being surveyed with darkness once again. The thought of everyone escaping entered and crowded her mind, due to the deep depression that she sensed surrounding Charlie, and from what she could tell, she has not slept. The thought of escape, the thought of freedom always crowds her thoughts in her mind. They needed to get out of here, and she wanted to help them as much as possible when that time came. At some point, it would happen. The thought of it happening was thin, but Michael could do it. He would open that door, and freedom would be waiting on the other side, along with the thing crawling around, but she would protect them with her life, without her offensive powers. That was an oath she made herself to God and swore to follow, and she would never break it. Her friends could get out of here. She would make sure of it. Millie wasn't able to go back to bed before she heard panting along with running slipping down the hall, then silence once a door slammed shut.

Screams, screams of fear, and agony erupted from the lab. Sally had been asleep at the time, but the first sound of crunching flesh had awoken her, and she was on her isolated bed in a small chamber.

Thousands of feet thundered down the hallway just outside of her door. Cries of terror weeping into the air. What was happening? Sally didn't know what to do, what was even going on. The voices sounded like scientists, people who had tortured her and everyone else in the large building she had been dragged into. By tall, scary men. She wasn't one of them and didn't know whether to follow them or to stay here, somewhere she had no idea if it was safe anymore. It never had been, but the sense felt even worse now.

Sally gained the courage to stand from her bed, slowly approaching the door that had gone silent. The screaming had stopped, she didn't know whether to think it was bad or good, all she could hear was her heart beating inside of her chest, pounding at the walls of her hurt stomach. Her hands shook violently, reaching for the knob of the giant door before herself. What should she do? Wait for an oncoming fate or go outside and see sooner?

She yanked the door open with all her might, not as slow as she anticipated, but it worked enough. Sally gasped in horror at the blood splatter, staining the pure white walls.

The girl slammed the door shut, backing up in fear with shaky breath. What was going on? So many questions stirred into a pot in her head, overwhelming her with countless ideas. Red is bad.

Red was really bad...was she left behind? Sally didn't know, and she didn't want to find out either of them. She couldn't sit here, she had to go, she had to leave and see what was happening. Or else whatever caused that blood was going to come after her too. That shook her to her core; what caused the red? If she stayed here, then it would find her. She had to leave, no matter what she told herself. No matter how scared she was...she had to go, right now.

She opened the door again and stepped out, keeping her eyes away from the red dots that formed on the wall, but eventually, she looked, and took a few steps back in shock. An arm lay lifelessly on the ground, coming from the inside of a door. She wasn't going to open it, her curiosity wasn't that stupid, yet it pulled at her, but she refused, she wasn't going to–

A roar came from the hall behind her, sending a painful sting in her ears that her fear prevented her from covering, coming from the hall that held countless rooms of children, or known as the Experiments to the scientists, and nothing more. She guessed she would know now, what had killed the person in the room. Sally slowly looked over her shoulder, her body carefully facing where the sound had come from.

Claws shanked themselves into the ground, bloody fangs dripping with red and drool. Sally's breath became heavy, matching the weight of her heart. A humanoid black figure taller than any other scientist she had seen stood before her. Malice and hatred were stored in its eyes. The tall figure stood in the hallway filled with mass kills. Anywhere she could've imagined, they were there, and that thing stood in the middle, covered in that very same blood from its victims.

The monster charged, crawling on all fours like some wild animal. She couldn't move; the creature had her frozen in fear, like it was keeping her there with glue on her feet. Was this acceptance? It felt more like terror to the point she was frozen into ice.

It was moving faster than any animal she could remember back home. She couldn't outrun this; it would kill her just as quickly. Sally shut her eyes, raising her arm and blocking her face with her hands, just to prevent the sight of bloody jaws coming for her head.

Her body was slammed into the ground, so fast to where she couldn't even scream, a protective arm wrapping around her stomach. It was painful but wasn't as painful as the death she was so close to experiencing. She watched as the thing launched into the air before falling into the ground just like her. A blurry figure out of her view but extremely close to her scrambled to its feet in front of her; she was too shocked staring at the monster to move, but she didn't have to by herself.

Sally was dragged off the ground, forced to her feet and already into a full sprint.

"Come on, Sally, we have to go!" an older but young voice told her. She couldn't see the voice until they were bolting in the opposite direction of the beast, passing the slain humans covered in their own blood, dead.

*Dead, they were dead. They were dead, dead, dead, dead...*

The girl gripping her hand tightly ran faster than she ever could. Sally tumbled on some occasions, but she certainly wasn't going to ask her to slow down, not when she heard the pounding of feet by that thing behind them, racing across bodies that it would probably devour. She didn't want to be one of the bodies, and she didn't want to think about it.

The other Experiment noticed as well, taking a quick glare at the thing chasing them. If it weren't for this girl, Sally would have possibly been dead meat by now.

The older girl spotted a dagger ahead as the corner became twenty feet away, taking a quick glance at the monster again, and then the weapon. An idea clicked in her head as she picked up her pace to enforce it. Her foot swiped once the blade was in range, and the dagger was kicked directly into her hands. She caught it and tossed it back like shooting a bow and arrow before Sally could even witness the event, quicker than any she could recall from television or real life for that matter.

The dagger speared the thing right in the leg. The thing screamed as it tipped over, landing face first into the stone soil, blood leaking from the open wound she herself decided to not look at for the better.

The two Experiments turned the corner; Sally being pulled into a room by the others' strength. Her hand was finally let go so the older Experiment could close the door quietly. A wisp of coldness whipped into her hand. She was given the chance to see the girl who had saved her life, only the back of her perfectly combed brown hair and dress that all the children wore though, so it wasn't that much of a surprise.

Sally wanted to ask who she was, but the fumbling of large feet shut her mouth fast. The other girl backed up to stand directly in front of her, placing a hand spread out of her position, a protective stance.

Once silence came, she still didn't want to say a single word, in fear that the creature would come back if it heard her tiny soft voice.

The older experiment turned to her, large worried dark blue eyes staring into her soul; they gave a feeling of fear, but also comfort. She breathed heavily like she was out of breath.

"Are you okay, Sally?" the girl asked, making Sally flinch back in shock. She didn't have a single idea of who the other thousands of Experiments were, not even one. How and why did this girl know her name specifically? And how did she now just notice?

Sally nodded her head. "How...do you know my name?" She clutched her hands together below her mouth as something to clench.

"It's one of my powers, I think—" The girl stopped her sentence right there, her eyes widening as she scooted past Sally.

"Excuse me for a moment." The girl stopped at the back of the room, crouching down and muttering something while reaching her hand out into a corner that she was unable to see. It was behind a shelf. Sally saw a figure as another hand laced over hers through the spaces in the storage equipment. The older girl asked if the boy that came out was okay, snot trailing down his nose with tears welling up in his light blue eyes and leaving his mouth. Suddenly, he leaped into her stomach and held his hands tightly on her back, just wanting to hug someone. He had probably wanted to do that for a long time; they all did.

The girl accepted it, embracing him as well as she looked back at Sally, lifting one hand towards her in an offering gesture.

"My name's Millie, and I promise to get you all somewhere safe."

Sally had awoken in her bed with a fright, jumping up and gripping the sheets with her fingers.

The screams still haunted her mind, to the point where she didn't feel safe in her room anymore. Safety wasn't there for her anywhere, so she ran, sprinted out of her room, and went down the hallway. Voices crept after her and into her ears; she had run as fast as she could into the dark, past the washer and dryer and to the first door that wasn't a room. She hadn't known what it was; she just wanted to get somewhere where she wouldn't bother anyone. Supplies surrounded her; she must have unknowingly found the storage closet. What was she doing? She was okay; nothing was going to get them here. Millie had said that. She believed her, but that monster's face continued to rot her mind. She couldn't think of anything happy anymore. Sally crawled into the back of the room, curling into a small ball while avoiding making eyesight with anything that was in the room, living or not, terrifying or not; she just didn't want anything in her sight.

A knock hit the door, a gentle knock, nothing of hurry to kill anyone...her.

"Sally? Are you okay in there?" Millie's voice was heard from the other side. She didn't answer, only letting out a breath of relief. The door creaked open, and Millie stopped in it, still holding the doorknob.

"What happened?" was all Millie asked. She didn't want to say anything at first, but eventually she built up the weary courage to speak up.

"A nightmare, about...the monster," Sally claimed, raising her knees in front of her face.

"Again?"

"Yeah..." Sally sniffed, rubbing a booger away from her nose.

"Sally, you will be okay. I promise, when we get out of here, I won't let it hurt you, and never let it get to you," Millie explained, extending a hand to Sally who was sitting on the other side of the room. "I promise that thing won't lay a hand on you."

*When.*

The way Millie worded things was complicated but...comforting. She always predicted something was going to happen, always told them that good would come, they just had to get through the bad events, only because of her faith. Everyone appreciated it; it gave them a small amount of hope, but sometimes it was barely helpful.

Sally got to her feet and walked over to Millie, taking her hand as her friend shut the door once she stepped out of the storage closet.

"I promise you; no one will let it harm you. He won't let it harm you," Millie said as they walked down the hall and to Sally's room, which wasn't that far.

Sally had a feeling that "He" was someone else. "Someone else" wasn't words she wanted to use to describe that "person," but she didn't understand much about what Millie believed in, even if she had told her some stories and "verses?" She remembered what they were called when Millie had spoken about some of them to her, to remind her to believe, and to keep her from being bored all day when Mitchell was done playing.

Sally crawled into bed on her own as Millie waited by the door before shutting it, but not before saying some final night words, "Goodnight."

"Goodnight," Sally said back, tucking herself into bed and flipping over to face the wall.

The room went black, and Sally lay there, staring at the ceiling for a moment before planning to shut her eyes.

*When.*

Millie always prayed to her God, Sally would hear her praying sometimes in her room, and sometimes in public with everyone else. No one judged her, of course; Millie had always said no to judgement of others. It was good advice, and everyone usually followed it. What was the point anyway? And Millie's prayers were mostly to get out of there in the day, and Sally hoped her God would listen, but what would happen if they did?

Has that thing died? If it stayed, it would most likely, but what if it didn't? How would they protect themselves? Millie's powers would kill her if she used them, the only one available was her "guessing names correctly" one, and then her healing powers, but those wouldn't do anything against something like that, but Millie always kept her promises. Though, she supposed there was more to the first than guessing names correctly. So, she just had to hope.

Would they even though? Sally had lost hope when Michael had tried for months to get that door open; Sally didn't even remember if it was months. Sometimes she feared when they were going to run out of supplies. She had asked Lisa hypothetically based questions about it, but Lisa had told her Michael would get them out beforehand, but it was obvious Lisa didn't even believe her own words. A lie, just a lie, Sally guessed she had borne the trait from her friend, Mitchell; the boy Millie had saved along with her.

After spending so much time with him, she had become him; they had become one mind at one point when playing together. The youngest children were the only two who played together, like the kids who played the games at parties while the adults spoke about whatever boring stuff they did or heard of in their lifeless older lives.

Sally wasn't suspecting the sudden sleep that drifted her away, and so her eyes closed into darkness.

Millie strolled down the hall. She had plenty of energy for this day, for this morning maybe. She heard muttering in the living room ahead, and a sigh left her throat. She knew that voice, the one she's been hearing every morning since they've been locked inside.

She walked around the corner and flicked on the light, Michael hissed at the flashbang. He was originally using a flashlight which he clicked off. He was crouching next to the door, peering into the hole.

"How long?" Millie asked.

"How long what?" Michael looked confused.

"How long have you been up?"

Michael went into an awkward pause before answering, "When I woke up at, like...three in the morning?"

"You really shouldn't be waking up that early, you know?" Millie said, leaning on the entrance to the hallway.

"I know. I just...I need to do this, Millie," Michael defended himself, determination lifting his voice.

"I know, Michael, but that doesn't mean you do it every single day to the point you are sleep deprived and starving yourself of food and water."

He darted his head over to her, just over his shoulder to see her. She sighed again, taking a deep breath when she saw the large dark eye bags mutating the skin under his brown weary eyes.

"We believe in you, Michael. You can get us out of here," Millie spoke her belief. "But I don't want you to get hurt because of it."

"I will eat, and drink. I'm not obsessed with this, or anything."

"You aren't, you're determined. You want to be the hero, and you are. Yet that requires energy and patience, and you aren't going to get much when you wake up at three in the morning every single day." She paused, "So please, for the love, get some sleep. Just wait. You will be shown the way when it is time."

A smile went across his face, a real smile.

"Thanks, Millie." She was about to ask for help, but he asked first.

"Are you sure, your powers are going to kill you? If you use them?" He confirmed for the hundredth time.

Millie nodded her head. "That's what I was told, by the scientists and so on. Even if I didn't believe it, I'd be on my own."

Michael had a skeptical look meant for her.

"Do...you want me to use it, to get everyone out?"

That question hit him like a freight train.

"No! Of course not! I was just asking." The panic in his voice was clear, along with the relief on his face after he screamed, like she would have done it immediately after if he didn't answer fast enough.

Millie had a sudden tense feeling, something of hope, but something that she would have to find to help Michael. She knew exactly who said it, but she just needed to find out what the words had explained.

The feeling drew her down the hallway, pulling her closer to where Sally hid last night. A door stood open to one of the rooms. A small, long yawn left Sally's mouth; she blinked like a frog with weary eyes.

"Good morning." Millie slipped the words inside before continuing to the close storage closet. She heard a quiet "morning" from Sally's room, but it faded as she moved to the upcoming door ahead.

Her fingers wrapped around the knob as she twisted it. The door creaking open in front of her as light poured into the originally dark room. Boxes of cans and whatever they needed to live sat still under mattresses, a broomstick and cleaning pan, pots and pans, and a bunch of other supplies. That wasn't what she was here for; the room was blacker than the hall outside, but the dim light on the other side of the doorway allowed her to see. Millie was told a secret, a secret neither her nor the others were told of for a while, and it was here. Now it was time to figure it out. This is what had been said to her this morning, and the sense wasn't a gut feeling...she knew it.

She walked over to the wooden walls, pressing her hands against it and grazing them across, checking for any bumps, anything out of the ordinary. It had to be here; it just had to be. He doesn't lie, or perhaps she went off in the wrong direction herself?

Millie stepped over a stuffed teddy bear; one Sally had stopped using when everyone believed she turned four. Her foot kicked a tennis ball next; one they hadn't used at all ever since they got there. The ball rolled across the carpeted floor, stopping at the wall. Something clicked at the contact made with the ball and the lower wall. A latch, disguised with the material surrounding her that no one had noticed in the dark room which giant boxes filled. Millie picked up her pace, coming to a halt and crouching down in front of it, examining the latch further. She had to get really close just to see it. No wonder they hadn't found this, something hidden in plain sight.

She unlocked the latch, pushing the small door that was hiding behind it. Nothing, so she pulled instead, and it flung right open. Inside was just darkness.

Her fingers were drawn in, and she felt dust, but dust that wasn't on the wall. Her hand rose itself across the mysterious object, and then it gripped a handle, which she instantly yanked out.

A red box with a black handle, a toolbox.

"Oh, thank you Lord, oh my gosh..." Millie gasped with relief. A toolbox, exactly what they needed. Oh my gosh, how had they *not* found this?

Michael was still working on the door when she stepped out of the hallway with a surprise gift. He looked back at her for what was supposed to be a second, and then he stopped and stared at her after spotting what she held, mouth agape and eyes widening.

"Guess what?" Millie glided across the room and set it down by Michael, who lifted the entire thing to just stare at it out of amazement.

"Oh my…thank you, so much! Where did you get this?" Michael thanked her with a wide smile on his face out of pure shock and gratefulness, lifting the lid to find so many tools, *so many...*

"Was this from that other power of yours?" Michael asked, chuckling.

"Nope." Hope, from God.

Charlie sniffed the morning air through her nose as she awoke from the peaceful sleep, the sleep that had gone by rapidly, like it always did. It felt short lived every time, but now she was just used to it. The girl yawned, instinctively hoisting herself straight to throw the sheets off, jumping out of bed.

The morning was quiet as Charlie strolled through the hallway, not even changing into her gown, or trying to grab it from the dryer. She forced her weary body around the corner, only to see Michael working on the door as usual, and Millie watching him from afar.

"Morning," Charlie burst out with another yawn, stretching her arms into the air.

"Good morning, did you sleep well?" Millie asked in her classic polite manner, yet Charlie didn't notice her giddiness nor excitement, nor the vibrant red box on the floor.

"I slept fine," Charlie stated, yet Millie knew it was a lie. She didn't know how Charlie was, or how she had slept, but the fact that she isn't jumping for joy at the sight of the toolbox shows she's too tired to even spot it.

"I am going to go get dressed," Charlie said, stepping back into the hallway, her footsteps echoing down the corridor until it was a small wisp.

Michael reached his hand inside, trying to get farther than before with the new toolbox that was miraculously found.

Millie watched from behind, eyeing him in case things went south. Nothing had happened to him, but a close call came once where he had almost shocked himself. He was fine, but Millie had watched him more closely afterwards, making sure to warn him of being extra careful, which he hardly listens to sometimes.

His hand was covered with the blanket of pitch black; she wasn't able to see his movements at all. He scooted his hand around with the only sense of touch, avoiding any wire he felt, but with every one there was another and another. He reached further, just as Charlie came back in the plain white dress they all wore that hung down to their knees. He continued reaching for the freedom that was thin, but possible. He felt the other side of the door, a cold wall. Pulling against the ache, he pushed his hand further. His palm hit it, feeling the smooth and cold texture. He had been right; the door that held them in the small prison was hollow but thin enough. He had reached the other side, the other side of the gate.

Michael plucked his arm out, scrambling into his toolbox. A handsaw was taken out. Millie stared at him with curiosity, watching him carefully with the dangerous tool. He shoved it into the door, and Millie smiled with realization once she remembered that the door was made of a softer material that wasn't the same as the unbreakable walls surrounding them. The people who designed the saferooms did not think their blueprints through. He started cutting the door like a piece of paper, feeling the tingle of the material falling to the ground on the inside.

He carried on, moving it up and down, left and right to fully cut the first barrier down. Soon, he had a hole in the door. Michael hoped it was enough as he set the handsaw down. His arm slipped back inside, his body moving with it. He was fully able to peek his head inside of the hole he had just cut, his hand hit the other wall again, this time he was able to see it.

Millie's eyes lit up; she noticed he was making progress. She watched him do his magic, every day, sometimes every night, waiting for him to finally rest. Millie lifted herself from leaning on the wall. Now, the kids might be able to, might be able to rest in a new bed, not the ones they have been laying in for years and years to come. There was hope, and that was Michael. He squirmed out, yanking the handsaw off the floor, careless about if it would hurt him or not. He moved it back inside, tangling it with all the wires that were hanging in the door, and then he hit the other side. He shoved the handsaw through the material and started carving a big enough hole; he didn't understand what it was big enough for.

*Just enough to fit a hand inside,* he thought to himself.

He could poke his hand through the other hole on the opposite wall of the door; his heart felt so heavy. It felt like it had left him for good, but it was still there. He just couldn't feel it thumping against his chest. He waved his hand around, looking for something, something to help them a little bit. Then he felt it, a doorknob. He moved his hand further around it, feeling what he thought might have been a broken lock.

"I found something! I found something!" he repeated with a shout, enough for everyone to hear, but maybe not.

Millie bolted towards the bedrooms, planning to wake everyone up from their deep slumbers; all of them would want to hear and see this. Charlie stood there in surprise at the words; those words felt so good to hear. Her dreams filled her head again; she could see the stars again, the moon, the sky, the sun. Everything was not a futile thought anymore. It could be real.

"What did you find?" Millie asked, running beside him after getting everyone up. She crouched down beside him, peeking through the hole.

All the children surrounded them shortly after, faith and hope they hadn't felt in years rising before them once again.

# Chapter Three

The Fight for Hope

Everyone was anxious and impatient, but they tried their best to keep their cool. All of them surrounded Michael. who was working hard, working for all their freedom.

Millie wiggled her hand around on the doorknob after Michael had asked her to try to unlock the door. This was it; this was their long-lost hope they hadn't known for so long. It had been lost, and Michael had found it. Finally, after all that time. They could finally be free, find a way out, and see the outside world for the first time in years.

They all heard a click, a click of something unlocking. Millie let go of the lock after twisting something she had no knowledge of. Millie pulled out her arm, standing up and placing a hand on the door. Michael stood up with her, looking for an answer on her face. She pushed, the door creaking open along with it. Everyone stood in shock, excited. Now was the time; they could finally be free.

Sally lunged forward, embracing herself around Michael.

"Thank you thank you thank you!" she repeated in high squeals. Michael didn't say anything back out of pure surprise. Lisa hugged him next, cheering his name as Millie joined in, then Mitchell and Charlie and Sally. They cheered his name, thanked him, for he was the key that just helped them escape this prison. After all of that was done, they prepared to leave.

"Stay behind me. Please, this could be dangerous. I don't want any of you to get hurt," Millie ordered. Stepping out of the door, Millie let herself hear everyone follow her movements, coming across a set of spiral stairs ahead of them.

Charlie watched as Millie peered down the stairwell, then she positioned herself straight. The girl turned towards everyone slowly, taking a deep breath.

"We can go down these, but it looks like some of them are broken at the bottom. We will have to stop at a certain floor," Millie explained.

They all moved closer, not having a second thought. The only thought going through their minds was freedom, and they were prepared to do anything to achieve it. It didn't completely control them; they weren't going to go insane, but they would do anything, absolutely anything, to be free. Millie started adventuring down the stairs, the rest of the group following her. Each step was closer to something they all thought was impossible, freedom. The group followed; they were anxious, wanting to see the outside world so badly, but to do that, they needed to be careful, to escape. Sally was one of the most excited out of the absolute joyfulness of the group, but then another thought pushed that excitement away, and gave her a new thought. One of fear and terror of that thing that might have survived off of the thousands of bodies for all those years, but Millie would protect them, right?

Being trapped in a small room for years without seeing the sky surprisingly didn't drive her insane. She looked up to the ceiling above her as they strode down; she hoped her dreams would come true, become the reality of her life, in all of theirs. This would be the best part, or the worst. Millie spotted the door to the level they were on, trotting over to it; she knew the stairs that continued would be in bad shape to walk on, so they had to end here. She tried to be as quick as possible, since she knew everyone, including herself, couldn't contain their excitement, none of them would, and they wouldn't really try to. A crumpled-up sign hung next to it, with the words still visible.

*Floor thirty–seven.*

She yanked the door open, the kids beside her looking past her shoulders in curiosity. Millie scanned the area before walking in; she wasn't relieved of her suspicion though, even when nothing was out of the ordinary.

She waved her hand as she continued further.

"Be careful in here," Millie warned. The place was in shambles, the ceiling was falling apart, rocks and glass were on the ground ready to splinter their feet, and no windows were in the area either. They hadn't let the kids see outside once, not even once. The kids were frightened of stepping on something sharp. Millie had to start carrying Sally on her back at some point, but nothing bad happened.

They came across doors, multiple, hundreds at least. A bunch of abandoned materials were also recovered, documents, and broken devices like the test tubes. The kids even found some reserved blood samples. Millie had held one for a little bit too long, about to crush the glass. It had almost shattered in her hand before Lisa had asked her if she was okay, and she let it go before she said, "Fine."

The group had been searching for more stairs that Millie had recalled from the past, then they heard something not of their own.

A roar, a shout of anger or surprise at the sight of something; Millie realized it was because of them. They froze in opposite spaces, each one of them looking over to where the noise was coming from. Most saw that it was behind a door, stable...at least they hoped so.

"Get behind me," Millie commanded without hesitation. Everyone listened, huddling together in a formation. A bang hit the barrier keeping them safe; a monstrous roar crawling from behind it. The thing Millie had worried so much about in her dreams, the one thing that haunted Sally for the past years in that safe room. That was it, and it didn't sound friendly.

The door burst open, a mist of fog rising in the long halls and rooms. It was like being in a sandstorm. It covered their vision blindly, not allowing them to see in the dangerous situation they had just set foot in.

Rumbles of footsteps shook the ground; panic arose among the group. Whatever it was, it was searching. The fear of it looking for someone stripped Charlie's peace instantly. That fear became true; a scream pierced the ears of anyone around them, a young scream, from the youngest person.

Then a fumble, and a roar of anger and frustration following afterwards.

Millie stood between the thing and Sally; she squeezed onto Millie's hand as some form of comfort. Its monstrous fangs created the tears rolling down her face, like she had done that first day of the horror she saw. The terror inside of her bones rattled them, yet it didn't scare Millie. She stood her ground, not letting her fear be the cause of her death or the others. It was human-like, as if it had been a human being before, but it wasn't now, and it was obvious. Its black moist body was seen after the fog cleared, making everyone turn in absolute fear. No one dared to scream, for it would only lead the monster straight to them. Its white glowing pupils met Millie's fearless dark blue. The girl didn't back down, now was not the time. It was a bad time to even think of giving up; her friends had waited so long to leave, and she wouldn't disappoint them, not when the thought of freedom was scrambling in every corner, every nook of their minds.

"Run," she whispered over to Sally. Sally didn't know what the feeling was. She had wanted to escape for so long, but leaving Millie behind was not on her list. Sally wanted to say something, wanted to reject the wish, but it felt so wrong. So, she shook her head, the only thing she was able to force herself to do.

"Go, now. Please, please, go," Millie pleaded after spotting her answer by the corner of her eye, keeping one slice of her attention on the monster.

It was at least twelve feet tall, having to bend down to fit in the room. Millie stared at Sally behind her with the corner of her eye, pleading for her to leave without words. The monster's long claws froze her in place. The thought of what it did to the lab that day terrified her. The monster itself made her not want to even live, but they couldn't stand here forever.

"Remember what I promised you."

For that to happen, she had to run. She had to listen to what was right, even when she was afraid.

That promise, one that Millie swore to follow, like all her promises. She always fulfilled them, and this one was no different. But Sally couldn't move, she didn't want to move, whatever she did, that thing would have a plan for it. None of the ideas were planned on sparing any of the children. A pounding headache was in her head, one warning, a sign.

"Run."

Sally bolted to her left, making the monster scream and lunge, but Millie ran forward as soon as the beast made its move. Somehow, she pushed it to the ground and slammed it, rubble rolling away from the collide. Sally had her ears covered; the scream the monster had let out pierced her ears. Everyone had heard Millie's words, yet Lisa attempted to stay back, to help her.

"Run! Go Lisa!" she screamed.

"Millie, I can't just leave you!" Lisa argued, but now was not the time.

"Just run!"

They followed Sally, away from the fight just like Millie had asked. Charlie ran at the back, having only a glimpse of the fight, only seeing Millie's brown hair before she got pulled out of her sight. She felt her heart drop when that happened, but she would only get Millie and herself killed if she tried to help. No, Millie could handle it; she was the most powerful Experiment. Yet her powers would kill her, but what about her strategic mind? Had Millie fought others for the tests?

The more powerful Experiments on the list were often tested on more, for their powers. No, Millie didn't have that type of heart to fight others, but she knew how to stand her ground. Her thoughts argued back and forth; she wanted to help, but what would it cause? What would it cost? Charlie didn't know, but she was so far away already with these thoughts. There was no turning back. The only thing she could do was follow Millie's orders and hope for the best.

Millie got slammed to the floor and held by the neck, the breath escaping out of her body. She felt blood rolling down her throat, moving onto the floor and surrounding her like a rain puddle. She gripped the monster's long claws, attempting to remove them from her skin. The thing pushed harder, forcing her into the unstable floor more, a spider-web of cracks formed around her as she saw the monster's arm start to shake. She was going to fall through the floor, thanks to the vicious beast. The floor was like a soft mattress, one that allowed her to be shoved further into the stone lines.

Millie watched as the monster's mouth opened, letting out a loud screech that shook the floor as an earthquake would have. She felt a hot liquid coming out of her ears, trickling down onto her neck. Millie tried to breathe, but the monster only clenched her neck even harder, forcing her to let out a gasp of air, and a stream of red. The crimson river covered her teeth like she was a vampire, escaping her mouth and flowing away, and she wasn't going to get it back.

Millie noticed a knife at her side. The monster's roar forced things to bounce from where they were. It gave her something, something to fight back with, something from God. She spread her free arm out, grabbing the knife's hilt and striking it into its arm. The thing screamed in pain, jumping back and gripping its arm out of agony and shock. Millie wasn't going to wait for it to gain an advantage. She rose up quickly, raising the withdrawn knife as she ran at the monster. Millie was only able to get close enough to skewer the leg before she got tossed back into a wall. She hung there for a second, before smashing against the floor, a piece of stone landing on her foot, trapping it and not allowing the freedom it needed. Millie heard the sudden noise, and looked back, only to stare at the unfortunate event.

She felt her vision blurring as she saw the black fuzzy figure running at her. Claws faced her to get a perfect hit. Millie struggled to break free, kicking her other foot at it to try and move it. Her toes wedged underneath and lifted it, throwing the rock through the air. She didn't look back at it as she rolled to her side, hearing the monster crash into the wall. The girl stumbled to her feet, having the courage to run.

Luckily, a natural tiny arch fell directly on her foot, leaving no damage to her foot as she ran. She didn't have energy left to fight anymore. A crimson stream went down her face. She already looked dead, dead as a corpse in a coffin. That's what she would be in if she didn't make it out of there. If anyone found her body.

"Please protect us, please..." her voice was hoarse as she prayed.

She turned a corner, not going in the direction the others went. She wasn't going to get them killed. That wasn't her job. She didn't know how someone could rejoice at the thought of having blood on their hands themselves, but she could never, and would never, do something like that.

Charlie and the others anxiously searched around, for somewhere to hide. They had found an elevator, but they wouldn't leave their friend behind. The group continued searching, shaking violently. One of them had started crying in fear. The thought of the pain that thing would cause them was large and painful to even think about.

"Over here," Michael whispered quietly, opening a door as everyone sprinted over, avoiding any rubble. They were all crowded inside the small room. Lisa slowly shut the door afterwards.

"Is Millie going to be okay?" Sally asked, her voice stuttering and worrying. Someone had to lie; someone had to say that she was going to be fine. That's what they wanted to know. What they wanted to hear, but...

"We don't know," Charlie choked out. It was hard to, but she had to; someone had to. Sally didn't say anything in response; they all sat quietly, none of them daring to say a single word to break the silence. Sally didn't realize she was holding her breath until Lisa nudged her and reminded her that it was necessary to live.

A small bed sat in the corner, which Sally curled herself up on; Mitchell joining her side. She was the only one he knew the most and felt the most comfortable speaking to.

A quick bang was heard on the door, making everyone go dead silent while holding their breath.

"We...didn't order pizza," Michael mumbled, intending to be a joke to make everyone feel better, but no one laughed. So, he didn't say anything else. Another soft bang was heard, causing everyone to jump.

"Hello?" Millie's voice was heard behind the door.

Charlie scrambled to her feet before Lisa could and yanked the door open, seeing the bloody mess Millie had become. Charlie felt the vomit filling up her throat. A gag came out of her mouth, she let Millie in. Who immediately went to a corner, covering her face to not let the kids see the disgusting mess she became. Even though she was covered in her own blood, everyone felt so glad that she was still alive.

"Do we have any bandages? Or something to cover the wounds?" Lisa asked around, but everyone shook their heads.

Millie turned her head slightly to where Lisa could only glance at her eye through the pools of blood down her face. Millie felt a pounding beat in her head; she would have to fight through it, even if she was about to almost pass out, but if she did, her healing regeneration should keep her alive.

Charlie vomited onto the floor, giving everyone a clear view of the green mush she threw up.

"Sorry, Millie...it's just..."

"It's fine..." she answered before Charlie could finish, with a comical smirk, "I understand. That is completely understandable, Charlie."

Millie couldn't be mad really; she couldn't blame her for being disgusted at all. She was full of her own blood, and some of the beast's was blended in with her own. The younger girl panted after finally releasing it, leaning on her knees while taking rapid breaths, attempting to focus on her breathing. Lisa ran up to her, but she brushed her off, since someone else had a bigger wound in the area at that moment.

They sat there quietly after a while, not even considering leaving the room. After a while, Michael spoke up,

"Millie," he called over, as she listened and walked. He held in the desire to release his lunch from yesterday while looking at the wounds Millie was covered in, but he continued, "There's an elevator somewhere, you think it could somehow possibly work?"

She sat down beside him, staining the white floor with red marks coming from her covered skin.

"It depends on how damaged it got during the attack. If it wasn't targeted, then maybe there's a chance it could still operate," she claimed, wincing at the pain in her side.

That was something everyone needed to hear, but at the same time, none of them could understand it. How could the machine operate after all the years the lab had been abandoned? It was impossible, but

Millie basically saved them. The reason they're not dead at this moment, or almost dead, was because of her.

Charlie took a whiff of the room and gagged inside of her throat. Gosh, Millie smelled awful.

# Chapter Four

The Elevator

Millie slowly pushed the door open. Nothing was heard, so she started to sneak down the hallway, gesturing everyone behind her to follow. They all slid on the wall as if they were on a thin cliff. Michael stayed behind Millie, pointing to where the elevator's location was. She listened carefully while also keeping an ear out for the monster.

They all creeped down a hall and soon reached where the elevator stood. It was damaged, badly. There was no chance. Their faces were covered in disappointment and lost hope, except for Millie, who had turned to Michael who coincidentally remembered something right at that moment. A memory that seemed to just occur as they made eye contact.

"Each floor had a starting generator, didn't it?" Michael recalled, searching the area for any sign of it.

"Yeah," Millie answered, joining Michael in peering down a hall.

The rest of the group felt unsafe, uncomfortable; they were in the open, completely vulnerable for any attack.

"Okay, so what do we do?" Lisa asked Millie.

Millie stood there for a moment. She didn't seem to catch the idea of no one wanting to be right in the open eyes view.

"I have an idea. Michael and I can go to find the generator that operates the elevators, and everyone else can find someplace safe near the elevator," Millie explained.

Lisa nodded her head, promising to not let her down. The rest agreed, since they didn't exactly want to be exploring.

The group parted their ways. Lisa put the others somewhere safe near the elevator, hiding them perfectly in a room where nothing or no one could find them. At least that's what she hoped.

Millie and Michael continued, hiding and stopping at any sound they heard. No one encountered the monster. Neither of the groups had heard it or seen it at all; not even a gut feeling had come up. The floor was quiet, too quiet. It had been silent for so long, almost painful to listen to the quiet shrieks of the abandoned ghostly lab. Something was bound to happen at some point. Millie and Michael would be prepared for it, and hopefully the others would be the same.

Charlie stayed silent, comforting Sally with a soft embrace, who was petrified of everything. Her tears were rolling down her face like a waterfall. Lisa paced silently back and forth by the entrance of the room, biting her nails while shaking. She was worried, worried like a mother. It was her brother's safety, one of her best friends' safety. Why was she feeling this? Millie would protect Michael, and he would protect her. She knew this, why was she so scared? Both would be fine, they'll be fine...yet those words didn't have the slightest bit of truth attached to them.

Lisa looked over her shoulder, watching as the others shivered. She was assigned to oversee the youngest by them, and she would do just that. She wouldn't let them down, people who hadn't let her down all those years they were trapped in the lab and the safe room. She had to pay them back once, the least she could do was this, to show she was worthy of being their friend. Or death would be the next option.

Michael trailed Millie, not even considering going ahead or leaving her side in the slightest. The halls were scuffed, full of rubble, dirt, spider webs, and their makers. Rats were heard ahead, squeaking and running across the mountainous floors, to Millie and Michael it was just kicking rocks aside.

Millie gazed around for a second before choking out blood that clogged her throat as she placed a hand on the wall, leaning against it with all her might. Michael stood beside her, forcing himself to pat her back in some attempt to comfort her, knowing his hands would be bloody from the choice he made. Millie glanced at him for a second, but it was all she needed to straighten herself and continue. She couldn't leave him and herself here; it would endanger them both.

"Why can't you heal yourself?" Michael whispered; it hurt him seeing Millie badly injured and *badly* was an understatement.

"My healing powers don't directly heal the injuries; they only stop the bleeding to keep the body alive," Millie answered in a whisper as they continued down the hallway, "and these are only stains. I can wash them off when we get out of here or find some place to rest at least."

"Calling it a 'healing power' is a little misleading, can you call it something else...maybe?" Michael suggested in a whisper. Why was he so frustrated by this, or was it some joke to make her feel better?

"I don't see a point. That's what everyone has called it," said Millie, "are you just trying to make us feel better?" A comical smirk stretched on her face.

"Yeah...sorry." He rubbed his head within the awkwardness of the situation.

She could hear the tap of the multiple legs the spiders wore when they crawled across the walls, the corridors, and halls. Millie saw an open doorway at the end of the hallway, so she picked up her pace, Michael keeping up closely behind.

The door was almost torn off, giving them no need to open it since they squeezed right through.

The room was full of knocked over shelves holding supplies, or what used to be supplies. Sitting at the back wall was the generator, covered with dried blood and a rotting smell. Michael swore to himself that if a dead body was here; he would just throw up. He knew it was insensitive and wiped that thought from his head. What was he thinking? That is so disrespectful...

Millie ran right through the smell and blood, passing it and allowing it to go to Michael. She examined the generator and all the gears, looking through a hole that led inside, having to brush off some spider webs. She even threw a spider out with zero hesitation. It zipped across the floor; Michael walked past it as it went in the other direction. He used to be afraid of spiders, but after spending time in the lab, he recognized that it wasn't the worst thing in the world.

"Do you know how to fix a generator?" Millie asked, wiping a spider web from a gear. Michael nodded his head when she turned to him and started searching for any tools.

"I should've taken the toolbox," Michael grumbled suddenly, moving scraps out of the way. He had forgotten it, how stupid could he be to leave something that useful behind? He guessed he was just too excited to finally escape the room. But he doubted he would be able to even run carrying something that heavy.

"It's alright. We could work with what's in here," Millie said. She didn't even try to blame him in any way.

Michael still scowled at himself for being such an idiot. Millie had left her bible as well, but when they got out of here, she could get a new one.

Millie moved a wrecked dead MacBook out of the way, only to find more trash; crinkling and rustling. She reached through and pushed it to the side. Her eyes widened in horror; she didn't expect it to be in a pile of trash. The place a corpse should never belong.

A skeleton covered in its own blood, surrounded by all the garbage, wasn't really the kind of burial anyone wanted after death. Millie drew her attention over to Michael on the other side of the room, checking to see if he was watching. He was busy scrambling through the other side of the room. Millie gently took the hand of the corpse, putting it against her forehead and closing her eyes, showing respect, something the person's soul hadn't been given for a while.

She slowly placed it back in the pile, grabbing a wrench that could be useful as she handed it to Michael who had walked over to her just as she covered the skeleton back up. There was no point in taking the body with them, the best she could do was offer them some dignity and her friend a remaining full stomach.

"I think this might be useful in some way," Millie claimed, avoiding staining the wrench red. Michael peaked inside the hole, checking all the gears, wires, and mechanics out.

"Somethings stopping it from moving. If I remove whatever that is, then I can get this working." Michael was relieved when he said that.

"So, it wasn't damaged?"

"Surprising, right?" Michael forced himself to move a spider web out of the way.

"May I ask for help?" He turned to Millie.

"What do you need?"

Lisa stood by the door, hearing for the sound of two pairs of footsteps instead of one. She didn't want to hear one walking; that wasn't good in any situation. Either, the monster was there, or one of her friends...she didn't want to think of that image. Charlie got up from where she was sitting once Sally had fallen asleep, stopping right beside Lisa to join in on her watch duty job.

Charlie didn't say anything for a while, only her heavy breathing was a sound cue.

Some words popped out, "You think Michael and Millie are okay?" Charlie wondered, asking Lisa about her thoughts.

"I hope so." Her friend's voice was shaky with every syllable.

But what if they weren't? What if that thing had gotten to them? Those thoughts crowded Charlie's mind. Feelings of fear and anxiety. Not what she wanted to feel, nor did any of them for that matter. Charlie's fists were clenched, clenched with anger at the thoughts plaguing her mind. Lisa spotted it with the corner of her eye, glancing at them for a couple of seconds before thinking of her brother.

"Sally needed reassurance before she fell asleep," Charlie claimed, wandering back to Sally. It wasn't really assurance, more of a comfort word, but it would do when she awoke.


Millie snuck up on Michael with the big flashlight she had found, along with the batteries she had placed inside. Michael flinched out of fear from her unintentional scare.

"Sorry," she apologized, scooting to the side and leaning against a wall, "need anything else?"

Michael clicked the flashlight on as he poked his head through the hole curled up in the covers of darkness.

"No."

He carried the cold steel wrench through, pointing the flashlight at a gear. The batteries she had found with the flashlight weren't that far off; she placed them in and thanked the Lord before returning to Michael, who attempted to work on the generator in the darkness.

"Did you do this all the time? You seem to be professional," Millie complimented, crouching down beside him.

"Well .... yeah, it's just one of my talents," he bragged sarcastically. He hit the wrench against the gear in hopes it would start spinning, yet it didn't. So that was not the main problem. The clogged gear was causing the rest of the gears to stop; he would have to fix it for the sake of all of them.

Michael continued searching, smacking all the gears and seeing which one had the stiffest reaction. There were hundreds of gears, each one of them capable of wiggling a little bit when they took the hit, but then one didn't. It took the smack like a beast; that was it. He waved the light over it, looking for the stopper.

A chunk of stone, sitting at the bottom and preventing the movement of one little gear. That rock must have been hard and stiff if it had stopped a giant machine from operating. Michael smacked the rock as hard as he could, knocking it directly out of the way. The gears moved again, causing Michael to dip as fast as he entered.

"Got it!" he shouted, but covered his mouth instantly, hoping to God that the thing didn't hear him.

The children were resting quietly when they heard something moving, like gears spinning against each other. It awoke Sally slowly; she joined in on the confusion.

"He got it..." Lisa muttered with excitement. She knew Michael well enough; he had done it. He had fixed the elevator.

The group retreated towards the machine, not wanting to wait another second before death consumed them. The elevator was almost gone, but was able to operate for a little bit, even without doors.

*It will only go down one floor,* Michael had explained, hating to ruin the excitement in everyone, but sometimes it was better to hear the painful truth than live from a comforting lie.

The group waited in the elevator, everyone hoping the generator would do its job so they could get carried to the next floor, hoping and praying that their end wouldn't find them. The numbers above the doorway brightened, revealing the floor to be thirty-seven still. A rumbling shook the elevator, crashing and cracking anything in its way. The shaking came to a stop. The numbers appeared back on the screen.

Floor thirty-six.

# Chapter Five

Another Distraction

Once the next floor was clear to them when the elevator stopped, they got out one by one. Millie helped everyone step over the giant crack that could've been the end of one of them. The floor was bigger than the first, but looked the same, with supplies still being scattered. Rocks and dust covered everything as the first layer of snow would on a winter day. The walls were full of cracks forming through the stone, crawling all over throughout the entire floor. This place had been attacked first; it had to have been. Either the monster started here, chased people up and murdered them, then made its way back down and continued the manslaughter. Savage beast. A craver that only cared for the power in its hands, and it hadn't even thought of the lives it took that day.

A fumble hit the ceiling above, possibly from the fall of something. Sally wished it could have been a rock, but she knew herself at six-years-old that there would be no way in the world that it was a stone.

The beast was running above them, the roof crumbling under its weight with every step. Rocks fell to the ground like an avalanche, shaking along the floor. Silence overtook them once the loud grumbles of stone stopped. The group stood there wondering what was going to happen next, and hoping what they were thinking wasn't going to occur in the next couple of moments.

The roof shattered like glass, rocks splitting Millie's skin open, her hands, her feet; it pierced through the outer layer of her body. She covered them all protectively, using herself as a body shield, but there was nothing. Nothing had come through the now giant hole in the stone roof. Millie slowly walked forward, leaning forward to see if anything was above; she couldn't sense anything but cold air spraying her in the face. The kids looked around, scared to even run. To move even, as if an invisible force held them down.

Suddenly another hole broke; the monster jumping down from it, swinging its claws attempting to hit what it was aiming for, but hitting Charlie instead of the intended target was not what it had planned.

The girl had jumped in the way, activating her power just in time to see it creeping over the young boy. She had shoved him out of his position, taking the full blow and protecting Mitchell with her face. The cut was deep, the hot dark blood pouring down from above her eye. If someone was going to die, then it would be her.

"Charlie! Out of the way!" Millie ordered.

The girl listened with a very quiet scowl, swerving to the side as Millie came charging through with a random dagger that had been left on the floor, piercing the things' stomach cleanly. It screamed, thrashing its claws around, slicing Millie in the face successfully.

She took a position in front of everyone, keeping herself in a stance in which anyway it would attack; the strike would hit her instead of everyone else. Millie pushed herself upwards, despite the pain. She was ready to fight again, even if she died this time, for her friends. She turned to see if Charlie was alright, but where the girl had been, it was now empty.

Charlie was gone, and that stopped her. She frantically searched around, trying to see where Charlie went while keeping her attention on the monster. Then a bang, clawing its way into the monster's ears. It growled in frustration as it turned to see Charlie holding a hammer next to a metal pole. She rammed it again, and the monster's irritated eyes faced her. Sally kept her ears covered throughout the event while letting out a slight mumble.

It lunged at Charlie, but failed as it watched her dodge, running away from the group, trying to get the thing as far away from them as possible.

"Charlie! That's a dead end!" Millie screamed.

She knew that; that was the plan. She saw the dead end at the end of the hallway, aware of what was behind it. The walls passed by her like she was in a car, fast and swift as her breath turned dull. The monster chased closely behind, jumping onto all four of its disgusting bloodied claws. The wall was a little miles away. A little bit more, then she could give them some time. Or were they even running? Was Millie following behind? Charlie had forgotten to consider it before starting the idea. She couldn't turn back, or a claw would go through her body. She picked up her pace, her breath retracting in and out from her throat heavily and quickly; fear grew her speed, fear grew her mind, her breath. It kept her forward, keeping her going. The wall was a few feet away, just a few more feet.

Her foot slipped, landing on the wrong side of a rock that flew behind her as she fell to the ground. Charlie scrambled to her feet, struggling to find a flat spot on the ground. Her foot hit the floor ahead, and she pulled herself up, bolting the rest of the remaining steps to the stone ahead.

She lunged forward, phasing into the wall like a phantom, a ghost. If she didn't keep this up, that's what she would become soon. The monster followed, fading through the wall and disappearing.

She had seen the monster above when it was about to attack, saw it run through the walls, then go through the next, watching them from below, eyeing them. It had the same ability she had been given, and she was about to take advantage of it. The shattering of the holes above was only an intimidation tactic, but that didn't work out so well for it. This was one way she could pay everyone back, some sort of way to help at least, just some way.

Charlie had gotten caught up in her own thoughts. Before reality hit her again, a slash went across her stomach, a stream of red escaping from her body, hurling her back to the real world of darkness. The blood trickled down her chest, causing her to breathe heavily in pain. She didn't have time to react before a second strike occurred, almost getting her throat, but it had hit only the lower skin of her neck, missing it by an inch.

She grasped it, attempting to distinguish the pain, but that wasn't possible. She was able to run before the third swing hit her, almost to the eye that time. Charlie leaped through another wall, slamming herself into the floor on the other side. She was quick on her feet, but not as quick as the monster who bolted through the wall, opening its long, sharp fangs.

The teeth bit down on her arm she had raised to block the attack; Charlie breathed a small sting of burning pain; she couldn't get back on her feet. It was holding her where she was, in a trapped position that would never allow her to run.

The monster smashed her against a wall; its claws inches away from sinking deep into Charlie's neck. Her throat ached with excruciating pain, badly enough to where she couldn't even let out a small rasp, to get a breath of rotting air from the jail she was trapped in. A small burn hit her throat; red left the area of the claw it had been holding her neck with. This was it; she just hoped her sacrifice would have a meaning and purpose for everyone else. Hissing came from its teeth; it was going to enjoy this.

Silence hit the monster like a whip.

A loud bang, hitting her ears like it was directly aiming at her, like it had shot her. Charlie felt the claws slowly unlatch from her neck, dropping her to the floor, flinching when the monster landed beside her, with a nice bullet hole in its chest. Charlie darted her eyes everywhere except over the body. Once she did, Millie was all she saw, still aiming the smoking gun that burned a short twisting line of smoke.

Charlie scurried around the body, running over by Millie.

"Are you okay?" Millie asked, placing a hand on Charlie's shoulder to heal her, since physical contact was all the wounds needed to stop bleeding. Millie's hand leapt off her shoulder as she started to trail down the hallway.

"The bullet isn't going to kill it, come on. Let's go." Those words caused Charlie to bolt after her in fear.


The two arrived back with the group, who were now in hiding again since Millie had run after Charlie without warning, only asking Lisa to hide everyone while her voice faded away. Charlie sat in the corner as soon as she got inside, hiding in her pain but also victory. Words started sprouting in her head, repeatedly. Why would she do that? Why would she even think of that...? The voice told her she could've gotten them killed, killed them all from that one simple act. Charlie knew it was herself, and that it would be better if she was...

Charlie turned her head against the wall, being able to see through them. The walls faded like ghosts, only leaving glowing remnants behind to remind her it was still there. She saw a machine, a machine full of gears, wires, and everything a generator would need.

"We have to get going, that bullet won't kill it," Millie said, the perfect timing.

"I see the generator," Charlie muttered, pointing at the wall like they could see it the same way she could.

She didn't look as bad as Millie did. Charlie had an appearance like someone threw wine on her minus the holes and scratches, while

Millie looked like she was mauled by a bear, but that thing is ten times worse than an animal. Poor Millie...

"Okay, so we're going with the same plan?" Michael asked; the entire group nodded in response.

Michael was on his feet immediately, ready to work on one of those machines again. It was a heavy burden, but he was willing to help, to take part in the journey to freedom, since he was one of the main causes for it, might as well contribute more.

It had been a little while later after Millie and Michael had left when Charlie realized something, one thing that was terrifying to know, and dangerous to realize this late. If it could see through walls and go through them like she could, then it knew all along. It knew where they were. It knew everything, tricking them into thinking they were safe, but no. It knew all along, and now that they saw it could go through walls, it wasn't going to be playing that game anymore.

It was going to go after Millie and Michael, attack them, maybe even murder. She had to warn them, had to tell them before their fate met them at the end of the line. She didn't know how far they had gotten, but she was going to find out. Everyone was sitting in the room, if she could manage to get out of that door, then…

Charlie bolted to her feet, running for the door before anyone could even see that she had lifted herself. Lisa was the first and only to react, sprinting after her in a worried panic.

"Charlie! Where are you going?" she shouted, but Charlie was already out of the door by the time she got to the center of the room. She heard Lisa shout for Sally and Mitchell to stay there, unaware of the risk she was taking with them.

"It can see through walls!" she screamed back at Lisa.

"What?" she answered back, continuing to chase. Oh my gosh...

Charlie kept running, guessing that the thing would go after Millie, the main threat out of everyone in this group, not two children that wouldn't cause problems for it, but it was petty. What was she doing? This was stupid, but they needed to know before...

The young girl sprinted down the hall, not caring to avoid any of the rocks that went through her foot. Blood dripped down her skin, spreading across the ground as she ran over the mountains of cobble, her feet aching from the constant scratching and slicing. She heard someone running behind her and knew exactly who it was. She had to lose her; it was such a big risk, but Lisa could run.

Charlie changed her direction suddenly, catching her friend off guard as she jumped into a wall, leaving the older one with no clue of where she went as she slowed her pace, her heart racing as she searched endlessly for Charlie, like she would appear before her again.

Millie handed Michael the flashlight they had kept. He turned it on, swiftly placing it onto the thin wall on the bottom of the hole, twirling the light around and searching for any problems with the generator.

"I can't tell, but it's not clogged by something. That's for sure," Michael claimed, placing the flashlight in his lap as he clicked it off.

"Maybe—"

Millie didn't have time to finish her sentence before a blood curdling scream came from the hallway. She recognized it, knew it.

"Get back to everyone else!" Millie shouted, praying to God that he knew where to go as a panicking pain was raised in her chest.

Another bloody scream emerged, this time, the sound of something spilling went afterwards. Millie ran towards the sound, her heart feeling like it had dropped down to the earth's core, praying to the Lord to protect her friend, to stop her death from finding her, to stop that scythe from attacking the young child that still had so much ahead of her.

Charlie was flown against the wall, the open wounds spitting out blood, dripping down her white gown.

She crashed into the cold hard ground, the red river moving through the canals between the stone.

Charlie felt her eyes closing as the twitch cornered her vision, along with the fuzz clouding her like the actual clouds in the sky. Her body shook with pain as she saw the black figure slowly approaching her, leaning over to avoid hitting the roof. Its white eyes were the brightest, not the thing she wanted to see when she died, but at least she was going to.

The monster bared its sharp fangs, a smile of glory spreading across its face. The end, an end of satisfaction on both sides of this brutal stop of life. Charlie's lips shook, a rose fluid leaking from her tongue and teeth. Anything inside of her was bleeding with aching pain. Her green eyes bled, the hot blood heating her face. Her hand lay in front of her, half of her skin covered in red. How had she not died yet? How was she not dead in the first place?

Millie sprinted down the hallway, rocks tumbling aside beneath her feet.

"Charlie!" she called, no one answered, *no one*. Millie picked up her pace, her breath heavy in her throat and stomach, thinking of prayer through prayer and holding her faith tight.

"Charlie!" she called again, still no answer.

Pure silence filled her mind. It felt like her heart was beating in her head, her brain was beating, her legs screamed in exhaustion. She fought through it and continued running. Resting wasn't an option until she knew they were safe, for sure, until Charlie was safe, safe from the monster.

She heard a snarl, a growl of victory, and achievement. No. No, no... please no.

Millie turned the corner, only to see the horrid sight of Charlie's body full of her own blood, not a single scratch on the monster standing before her, ready to strike. A sense of emotion washed over her as she ran towards the beast without hesitation, a feeling of urgency rising. She wanted to protect, she needed to protect them, all of them.

"Hey!" Millie shouted, hoisting a nearby dagger from the ground.

The monster had no time to turn around before the blade went straight through its chest, a hiss of pain escaping as the dagger tore through its flesh. Millie didn't stop there. She stabbed again, splintering it's side that time. Charlie watched in horror as the thing threw Millie back, but she didn't quit. The kid charged, taking only a brief second to get back on her feet. The thing swung a claw in front of it, but missed by a second as Millie ducked, leaping to the right as she yanked the knife out of its side, then quickly jumping onto its back like a ferocious animal, clinging on as she raised the now red steel and stuffed it into the neck, blood spraying in her face.

The thing ripped Millie off its back and tossed her, slamming her into the ground at least ten feet away from it. The claw raised towards the weapon, slowly gripping the hilt sticking out of its neck, and yanking it out with no hesitation. Millie froze at the sight she saw next.

She watched as the skin of the neck slowly molded itself back together like it was alive, covering the bleeding wound.

It had a healing ability that didn't make them feel any better. Millie whipped her vision towards Charlie, who was almost dead, but still alive, alive. She was still breathing, her heart still beating in her chest, a miracle from God. It rolled its head back over to Charlie; something snapped inside of its neck as it moved.

It cracked, popped, or broke; either one of those wasn't any better than the last.

Charlie tried to get up, tried to move, but her body was numb, covered in her own blood. She was going to die, there was no chance she could survive this, right...?

"Charlie!" Lisa's voice was heard down the hall. She could make out it was Lisa, even though her heart felt like it was thumping in her ears. Charlie swore she could see the afterlife coming to take her away and move on from this miserable life she had gone through.

She was so sorry for this. For all of this...

Lisa bolted past the corner, only to stop in fear, and pain for the two horrid sights laying in front of her. She saw the mess of blood that the thing had turned Charlie into, worse than what Millie went through in the first fight. The monster whipped around, facing its attention towards Lisa. The girl looked at Millie, then Charlie, two poor innocent souls, about to die in the most gruesome way possible. Alone together.

She had to do something to get it away from them.

"Yeah! Come and get me. Slow demon!" Lisa taunted unexpectedly.

The monster seemed to understand her. Its white eager eyes fully focused on her; her small reflection stood in the glow, defenseless, but with a risky plan.

Lisa whipped around, running as fast as she could down the hallway she had come from. The monster was bored of Millie and Charlie; the two were already half dead. The other was fully intact. It fell onto all fours and galloped after her.

"I got it! Go help Charlie!" Lisa shouted as she ran, even though the feeling of upcoming doom made her voice shaky and fearful, but she continued running.

Millie trusted Lisa; she could handle running for a little while. She stood up, keeping herself upright as she walked over to her friend. Millie saw the twitch in Charlie's green dull eyes; she was still alive and breathing. Millie crouched down by her friend, placing a hand on her shoulder.

"Charlie," Millie whispered, gently shoving Charlie's body; her hands were instantly filled with blood, Charlie's blood.

"Come on, Charlie, please. Fight it, get up," Millie pleaded, her voice shaky with her own pain as she activated her healing power.

Charlie still couldn't get up. She wanted to listen, wanted to make up for her mistakes, and now they were here, both almost dead, because of her. If she died some time. She could face the consequences of her actions for staying quiet, for not listening, at least she would pay for it.

The pain rotted against her; she already felt dead, felt like a corpse, but Charlie was even worse. She couldn't complain, she had to get them to safety. Yet where was there safety in the forsaken dump they found themselves stuck in?

Millie moved her hand under Charlie's arm, pulling it over her own shoulder to keep her upright, before getting up herself.

Millie started moving, dragging Charlie along with her, moving slowly for the sake of her friend. The pain in her legs was unimaginable, but she pushed forward, fought through it with a shield and sword, tossing every single last one of it out of her way. She just had to hold onto Charlie and get her back to the room with everyone else.

"Please help us, please..." Millie mumbled as the two limped through the hallway.

Lisa scrambled around the corner, almost tripping over only God knew what. Her black hair was waving behind her, flopping and twisting. She had been running for so long; her feet were starting to fail on her. It felt like she was going to die of it; she was so tired, but she had to keep pushing for Millie and Charlie. Those words were in every single sentence of her mind at that moment. *Millie and Charlie, Millie and Charlie, Millie and Charlie...*

Lisa's pondering got the better of her, causing her to accidentally ram herself into a wall; her legs too focused on running to try and switch her direction. Lisa immediately gained her focus, moving and ducking out of the way as the monster jumped through the wall, meaning to get her instead.

Stumbling around the rubble in her way, she kicked some into the wall to move further. She didn't know how to stop the pain. The ache in her legs was excruciating, exhausting, painful, but she kept going. She had to; she just had to keep going.

All the kids' eyes widened with horror as they saw Millie and Charlie stumble in.

"Press pressure on the wounds! I'll be back!" Millie shouted, bolting out of the room. She noticed Michael on her run out and had heard the rumbling from the generator. He had fixed it when she left, good, one other kid to not worry about.

Lisa was still out on the floor, running for her life, running until she collapsed from exhaustion. That was something Millie didn't want to picture.

It was all her fault; she was the reason she was even like this. She was the reason Millie was on the verge of death, and Lisa as well, two people, all because of her? All of it was because of her, all the accidents, the pain, the torment, it was because of her. She deserved to die. Charlie sat as she laid out an arm for Michael, who started bandaging it with cloth from a medkit. She would have asked herself how she wasn't dead, but she already knew the answer.

Millie felt like her legs were going to burst, but she wouldn't stop even if that happened. If it even could happen. Lisa wouldn't be in much trouble if she just used…

No, she wouldn't leave them alone.

She felt a gut feeling in her chest, not the pain or fear, but a feeling, a feeling something was going to happen, a warning.

Millie looked around, searching for any sharp objects she could find. A sharp dagger was lying on the ground. It was rusty but still could cause fatal damage. She yanked it off the floor as she continued sprinting, gripping the sharp weapon in her fingers. She heard a rumble, a bang, almost like an explosion.

This was it, the *gut* feeling.

Millie raised the knife as the monster came hurtling through, holding Lisa's neck in its claws. Millie sent the blade straight through its gut, a blood leaking scream shriveling their eardrums.

It dropped Lisa, sending her tumbling to the sharp, stone floor. She lay there motionless for a second, but before she knew it, Millie had yanked her body off the floor and helped her get her to her feet instantly. The two bolted not long afterwards, the pain in their legs suddenly just giving up. Millie noticed Lisa clumsily stumbling over the rocks, so she gripped her hand while she ran, in case she tripped. The monster started on all fours again, leaping over each step swiftly, crushing each rock after every land, the remaining pieces rolling across the mountains of rubble. It was catching up so easily, so quickly.

It lunged to the wall, digging its bloody claws in deep as it continued the chase on the stone holding the kids in.

"Are you serious? It can run on walls?" Lisa screamed in annoyance, her fear overwhelming her voice in a shaky tone.

The thing roared; a piece of anger it had been holding in for a while. The scream had been an answer to Lisa's annoyance, her anger, throwing the screeching rage right back at the girl that it had used to envy so deeply, out of the hundred kids, but not anymore.

They were near the room, the room full of the rest of them. They couldn't lead the thing in there; they would all die, and Charlie could barely walk at the moment. It wouldn't end well.

Millie suddenly stopped, not a fraction of friction in it.

"Get the kids to the elevator!" she yelled to Lisa, preparing for the impact of the monster's attack. The thing threw her back, the blood from the scratches ripping away from her.

The monster opened its mouth, the long slithery tongue hanging out of its mouth like a panting dog. The fangs were hiding behind, revealing themselves as they opened for the bite. Millie jumped out of the way, her body frantically trying to gain its step, but it couldn't, slamming her into the wall, her shoulder taking the full hit.

Millie was able to catch her steps again, running in the opposite direction of where the elevator was located. She knew the place; she remembered exactly where the halls were, the floors, rooms, everything. She would be able to circle around, if she could stand her ground and survive; she would be fine. She checked behind her, only to see it carrying on her chase. Good, that's exactly what she wanted.

She forced her legs to move around the corner, using the wall as a brace as she examined the hall ahead of her, at least twenty doors, and another corner at the end. Two more rounds to go, and she would be back at the elevator, great. She bolted through the hall, as fast as she could. The corridor felt like it went on forever. She guessed she would've passed a hundred doors by then. Millie continued running until she could touch the end of the wall. It was sharp, but she held it tightly to avoid falling out of exhaustion.

The monster's multiple footsteps echoed down the hall. She turned back, only to see the fuzzy figure zooming towards her. It was enough to get her moving again, sprinting down the next hallway. It was another long and sharp one; one she knew would feel like forever until she hit the end of it. It would be a death sentence, but she placed one foot after the other as she carried herself down the long and endless prison.

Running, dodging, keeping herself up was a challenge enough in itself, until the monster roared again, shaking the whole entire floor, causing her to tumble and fall, but Millie kept running once she got to her feet. She told herself to just keep going, to get back to her friends. Their safety was a big priority, her mission, her only thoughts. A mission she promised to her Lord. The only thing she would fight for was her friends, for they were her world.

Lisa waited anxiously by the elevator, her eyes frantically taking in every detail of each hallway. Every sound that went into her ears, every gut feeling. Everything felt important at that moment and caught her attention, even the sound upstairs. The rats that ran across the hills of rocks, the canyons. Everything, *everything*. The rumble had knocked her down; she hoped it hadn't caught Millie off guard that badly.

A rock rolling across the ground moved around the corner. Squinting down the hallway, she saw the figure of Millie running down the stone hall, more footsteps rushing behind her.

She stumbled, tumbling around due to the agony of the wounds on her body. The monster's chattering gallop was right around the corner; how long had it been chasing her?

"Get in the elevator!" Millie choked out from down the hallway.

Lisa obeyed, despite knowing this could end badly. All the kids were pushed into the elevator right at the command. It was large enough to fit all of them. Millie picked up her feet.

Fifteen feet, her legs felt as if they were about to explode.

Ten feet, her breath died on her.

Five feet, her legs were giving up on her as she watched as the doors started to close. The monster's breath was right down her neck, the hot breath lingering over her skin. Her friends cheered her on, fear in their voices as they watched the unstoppable elevator doors closing.

She lunged, squeezing perfectly through the doors. Everyone got out of the way, either running or placing their backs against the wall. Michael, who was planning on catching her, refused to do so. He wasn't fast enough as she slammed him into the wall with her whole body unintentionally. Millie looked over at him, her dark blue eyes glaring at him through the waterfall of blood.

"Are you okay?" she asked, just processing that she had landed on Michael while she crawled off him.

Michael stared at her with a shocked and at the same time, concerned expression.

"I should be asking you that, but for clarification. I am fine. Now are you okay...?" he said, sarcastically as she rested against the wall.

"For now, yeah..." Millie spotted Charlie in the corner below the broken elevator pad. Her green eyes were full of guilt, almost lost of color; her wounds covered with bandages.

Charlie scooted a medkit over the floor that the group had taken from a room they had found, unsure if it was even going to work, but they didn't have free access to a hospital right now; the medkit was their only hope at comfortability.

"Thanks," Millie muttered, opening the lid of the red box.

They had gotten almost killed, thanks to herself, and they were almost dead. How many floors did the building have? How much more would they have to go through to reach freedom? All these questions flooded her mind easily with the tsunamis of words. The answers she didn't have and probably would never have if she continued to keep quiet.

Millie had always told them to have faith, keep their hope, but they hadn't listened, but now they had it once again. They were almost there; it's as if she knew what would happen, like she knew they would have existed.

Faith is now in their hands again, hope was flooding the inside of their hearts. They had it again. Hope now contained them, and they would fight with it. Fight with a shield and sword and wouldn't stop even if they broke. It was a fight for their freedom, and they weren't going to give up, not until they would all sleep peacefully in a bed, knowing that outside was waiting for them in the morning.

# Chapter Six

The Chase

The dented doors slowly slid open, the numbers thirty-five slowly phasing into the blank black box, symbolizing the end of the hopefully safe ride.

They exited, preparing for another chase or hiding spree. Charlie had forgotten to warn them that the thing could see through walls; she should have told them by now. The thought had just popped up back in her head.

"It can see through walls. Sorry, I forgot to say," Charlie warned, finally able to get it out of her mouth.

"Oh, so hiding is not an option then, great..." Michael scowled, dramatically letting his arms fall to his sides.

The others stared at him, not falling into the temptation of his humor. Millie doubted it was supposed to be funny, though.

"Now is not the time to be making jokes, Michael," Lisa joked, nudging him by the shoulder.

As his sister walked away, he retorted, "I wasn't trying to."

"The safe rooms are still an option. If Charlie can't get through those walls, then it shouldn't be able to either," Millie pointed out.

A wave of relief washed over everyone there.

Sally stopped behind Lisa, staring down the hallway with her upgraded vision out of curiosity. She felt a breeze rush through her, a brush of wind running past her and into the people in the back, giving them a crisp chill of the cold outside. Though Sally had no idea where it could have possibly come from.

"Should we start finding the generator?" Michael suggested, his voice full of a tone of awkwardness.

"If there is one, they might have changed it up halfway through the construction, because they were just unpredictable like that," Millie sighed.

The room was silent as they started traveling through, looking at every open door they found, and slowly opening some. Michael hadn't followed along with that pattern and had accidentally knocked a broken door down, sending the sound of clashing metal to the entire floor. Everyone's heart beats went to their stomachs after that.

Silence cornered them, the only sound specifically being the crunch under their footsteps. That thing would surprise them, attack once again. Everyone knew that, but they ignored the thought, pushed out the warning out of fear, except Millie. Despite being the most injured, excluding Charlie, she was still willing to fight, fight for them, and fight for their safety. They meant the world to her, and losing one of them would be the end of it, all of it.

Millie left that thought behind, not daring to even consider if that could happen. It wouldn't happen. She wouldn't dare let that happen. If that beast ever hurts them, then its body would be torn from limb to limb. She didn't even want to think about it, but whatever was keeping it inside these walls. It would break out of that, and it would hunt them down to the end of the earth.

They heard a stomp that wasn't their own, circling back to the floor above. The thing was playing that game again. The black humanoid beast ran on the ground over their heads. The sounds of the footsteps quick and swift, easily scavenging, moving like a predator through the tall strands and lines of rocks in the halls. Its footsteps started going in a circle, directly where their heads were.

It had found them. It knew, and it would certainly jump down to kill them all. If not there, then somewhere else.

The group started running, their hearts thumping in their chests as they heard the footsteps following their every move. The thing gurgled above them as they ran, licking its slimy tongue around its mouth. Sally could hear it do all of that, and it made her want to vomit. She let out a gag at the sound of it, trying her best to keep it inside. The noise stopped, no sound could be heard from above, even Sally couldn't detect anything. Millie felt a warning in her chest, a feeling. The group stopped, searching the place for wherever it was dropping, for they knew that no matter where they were going to run, that thing would know their direction and surprise them. They already knew the rules to the game now.

The ceiling exploded where they were originally heading. The stone crumbling to the floor as the black figure lunged, grabbing Millie by the arm.

"Run!" she shouted.

Its large fangs bit down through the bandage, soaking it in a red splatter. The rest of the group bolted, obeying Millie's command.

She struggled, tossing her arm around viciously. Millie searched for some space for her feet, but she got slammed into the floor instead, the thing's teeth remaining in her arm. Millie let out her free one, grabbing the biggest rock she found, and swinging the sharp edge of the stone into the white glowing eye. The monster opened its mouth and out went a painful scream, tears of blood pouring down its face.

Millie released the rock, carrying the white orb with it, and a red moist cord of flesh that slithered along the ground. The texture was wet and disgusting; her foot kicked it away, like she was giving the monster its eye back. The thing still stood over her body, like it had frozen. Its chest still rose and fell. Was it alive? She had no idea anymore even though it still breathed. Millie forced herself into an open area, freeing herself from being under the long thin body, scrambling to her feet as she ran around, getting it as far away from the kids' direction as possible. Millie didn't plan to take the eye out, but it was good enough. The wound had bought her some time, along with the others. She heard the screams of pain fade into nothing as she ran farther away from it, hoping it saw where she went, and not her friends.


Charlie moved on the urge of collapsing; her whole body quivered, shaking with some of the blood that escaped from the tight bandages. She continued moving, the wounds throbbing and aching.

Her legs collapsed before she could realize it, causing her to fall into the stone's hard floor, smashing her head against it. The wound on her forehead opened, the blood leaking from inside the bandage.

Michael noticed and stopped to help her.

Her wound was opened fully, the blood pushing through it as it dripped down her face. She breathed heavily in fear, a drop of blood crawling back into her mouth. She spit it out, the tears drooping down her face as she cried silently in pain. Her green eyes welled up with droplets of sadness, falling down her face, more rising in her bright eyes after the other.

Lisa and the others watched in horror as the bleeding got worse. They had forgotten the medkit in the elevator, how had they just realized that now? She looked around, looking for some sort of medical pack. She saw a gray sealed door, like the one in the safe room. Lisa realized it as well.

"In here!" Lisa called, opening the door to the safe room.

Everyone didn't hesitate to bolt in. Lisa was the last to enter, the door fortunately locked from the inside, unlike the first safe room. The room was exactly like the first, a kitchen, living room, everything, but they weren't there to stay. So, Michael ran off into the safe room, sprinting to the storage closet to help Charlie.

Lisa stood by the door, waiting for Millie to come and join them; at least she hoped Millie would. The hall was silent; besides a squeak she heard outside, definitely from a mouse.

Michael ran back out with a medkit swirling around in his palm. Charlie held her head tightly with her hands; she didn't know what to do, what to think. The amount of blood loss was so severe that it clouded her vision and her mind.

Michael had to unwrap the bandages, had to remove the white cloth from her head. He gulped, quickly taking the bandages off her forehead. The blood immediately spilled out, the pain increasing for the poor girl every second, every moment.

The procedure was long, and painful, but eventually they were able to replace the bandages and care for the wounds. Charlie had passed out right as she collapsed onto a bed in the room, exhausted from it, from everything. She curled up on a blanket in one of the rooms in the back, similar to her first room. All the safe rooms they had been in looked the same.

She snoozed soundly and peacefully; the room was cold, but the blanket warmed her like the star outside that they hadn't seen in years. They all sat quietly in the main room, besides Lisa, who was still hearing for Millie through the door.

"Is Millie okay?" Sally asked, her voice full of innocence and worry.

They all looked at each other, no one even considering answering the question.

"She'll be alright. You know Millie, she's a strong girl," Lisa reassured, her smile obviously fake. She just hoped her words were right.

Sally didn't buy it. Even though she was six-years-old, with the amount of death and life situations they had gone through, she couldn't believe anything or anyone anymore. Sally played with the two buns

Millie had tied into her hair, the same girl that everyone pleaded for to be alive.

Suddenly, running footsteps sprinted across the floor outside. It was two feet, not four.

"Millie?" Lisa whispered through the door, praying that the voice she heard wouldn't be a roar.

"Lisa?" Millie's voice answered, the quiet stepping of feet stopping.

Lisa yanked the door open, seeing the bite mark of Millie's arm.

Millie walked inside, seeing everyone resting around the main room, besides the badly injured Charlie.

"The door locks from the inside. We will be able to open it," Lisa said, closing the door as Millie turned to her, clenching her arm tightly to fight the blood leaking through the spaces between her fingers.

"Where's Charlie? Is she okay?" Millie responded to Lisa once realizing Charlie wasn't with everyone else.

"She opened one of her wounds, Michael put on different bandages." Lisa scanned the hallway like Charlie would walk out of it good as new. "She's in one of the rooms sleeping, probably the same one from the first."

Millie waited for her to finish before going to the location Lisa had described. Millie slowly peeked through the small crack in the open door. Charlie was resting, new bandages all over her arms, and certainly over her whole entire body.

"It wasn't just the wound," Millie revealed, letting go of the doorknob as she left it open a little.

"What do you mean?" said Lisa.

"She used her power too much," Millie explained, holding the wound tighter, "it exhausted her. Basically, she overworked herself."

The conversation went quiet for a second, before Lisa started it up again. "Are you sure you don't need any help?"

"No, you have done enough. We should just rest for now," Millie assured.

Lisa peered down at her bandages worryingly. She hated that Millie was like that, but she wouldn't try to change her mind because of her own thoughts about it. Millie started a short walk further down the hallway where they had put the medkit, knowing that Lisa was staring at her stroll with her dark, concerned eyes.

The red box sat on a bunch of rolls of toilet paper. Millie gripped the handle, taking it off and opening it. She didn't want to make everyone watch her heal herself, so she rested down on the floor and opened the medkit, starting to unwrap the worn-out bandage on her head. The kids were going through enough already. Seeing open wounds wasn't a surprise to them at this point in their lives, but still, just because they were used to it, didn't mean they wanted to see another.

They had gotten through three floors at least, and they had almost died. How could they possibly be able to make it through the next? And the remaining floors that seemed endless?

If she used the remains she bore, maybe…

No, the fight wouldn't be a guaranteed win.

The team would, the kids won't give up in this fight. This building was holding them back from freedom. The outside world, the stars, the sun, the moon, the trees, rivers, other civilizations, everything that was on this earth. They would escape, and it would be worth it. God would guide them through the building, protect them from the monster, one possessed and tempted by the devil. Even if death would almost hold them, even if she died. Those kids would get out, no matter what, even if it cost her life. Their lives were more important than hers.

# Chapter Seven

Healing

Their time there had been forever. An infinite loop that pulled them back inside at any chance of escaping. Even though they had each other, every last one of them wanted to see the outside world before they left the earth. No one wanted to die in this hell.

As the blood was soaked into the bandages, it was blocked from going any further out of the wounds. She had a sense of relief rush through her, feeling free of the pain from the attacks, from the monster who had once been man. She remembered him, one who had the emotions of selfishness corrupting him, one who craved power that he couldn't get on his own. Stealing one from the lab was his next option, and he took it. Deep down, inside the beast he had morphed into, he knew what he had done, and he didn't regret the decision. Millie left the seat she took on the floor and found her way back to the door, twisting the knob and getting flooded with blinding light that her eyes were not used to seeing after so long in the dark.

The door creaked open, and Millie exited through it. The bandages would hold firmly; she hoped they would.

Millie stopped by the room Charlie was in, still soundly and peacefully asleep, her chest rising and falling, a sign of a soul still in the body.

Charlie slept, her mind in darkness, silence. Time flew by in her head, almost coming to a close before she woke up. Her breath was slow, painless.

Stuck in the dark, alone, tired, sad, crying, her green eyes watered as she curled up. Her vision not being able to adjust to the dark ahead. Alone, tired. Tears rolled down her face; she couldn't handle it. Couldn't take the pain anymore, all of it, the darkness...

Her eyes were pulled open, taking in the darkness of the room. Charlie felt like panicking, but she clumsily turned on the lamp beside her, the light slamming into her face. Darkness felt so wrong now.

*Wrong. Wrong. Wrong.*

Charlie felt tears rolling down her face. Darkness, tired, alone, taken, abandoned. She stuffed her face into the pillow, the water staining it into a dark platter. Her teeth didn't let go of each other as her lips quivered, to keep herself quiet, like she always did, keeping her pain, her sadness to herself.

Why? Why did any of this happen? Why was she here? Why were any of them here? The courtroom, the picture flooded her mind; those words were haunting, all of them were, the voice itself as well. Even if she wasn't there, even if she wasn't there to plead the case, that sentence haunted her like a vengeful ghost.

*I hereby sentence you to death.*

Those words pounded at the door to her thoughts, yearning to be let in and torture her. Torture her until nothing was able to handle more inside. Butterflies turned and twisted, yet no sign of worry infested her; pain was all she felt, pain, emotionally and physically. Pain, just pain.

Millie had noticed her crying for a while but had left her alone. Charlie would appreciate not mentioning it, so Millie would respect that. Though Charlie shouldn't keep doing this.

The red spots from crying under her eyes were still not absorbed back into the color of Charlie's skin. It was obvious, but no one seemed to notice beside Millie. Now, it was time to move on, move back into the nightmare that fighting to get out of was more of a necessity at this point.

Millie stepped forward, slowly opening the front door. The children wished it would have been that easy during those years.

Michael had worked all that time to just get that door open, and he had done it, but he always wished that door could just open with a push, a simple push like how any other door would work, but the place wasn't simple. If death and murder counted as "simple," then the lab would be all the way at the top of the chart.

Millie peered out of the doorframe, examining the area, searching, but nothing was found. So, their journey went forth, walking through hallways, searching through some room after curiosity got the best of them, and stopping at the slightest noise that shook every single one of them to their core.

Soon the generator was found, ready to be fixed in a small room at least five hallways away from the elevator. The cords had somehow disappeared, so they could only rely on Charlie's abilities.

Michael poked his head through the generator, a disgusting smell stabbing his nose. It was so bad that he had to leave the hole every few minutes. It made him want to clog his nose and just die. The generator reeked of dust and spider webs along with what God knew what.

The thing was soon operating again, the gears swirling and twirling, dancing around with each other. Michael got to his feet, turning towards everyone and giving up a smile while putting his thumb up in achievement. Everyone wanted to cheer, but they had to stay quiet, pure silent, quiet as the wind on a slow day, quiet as the death of a flower.

The group had started to creep towards the elevator, the halls in complete silence, rocks falling from the ceiling, finally leaving the stone overhead after hanging on for so long.


A screech echoed down the hall behind them. Each one of them whipped around in sync at the sudden noise, all expecting to see the beast scrambling towards their group, but it was just nothing.

Another echo erupted in their ears. It was the monster, still screaming in pain from Millie's brutal attack. She didn't regret it a bit, didn't even intend it, but it definitely hurt since it sounded like the beast was burning alive in the deepest pits of hell.

Millie had convinced everyone to move forward, assuring them they had a little bit of time to get as far away as possible. It wouldn't be able to harm them anymore, at least for now.

The elevator felt smaller than usual, but it was still the same size. That feeling had just popped up in Charlie's head for some reason. The machine moved on, smoothly leaving the floor of the monster's screams of pain.

Next floor, next journey, next fight. This floor had felt quick, swift, and peaceful. After Millie's blow, the monster seemed weak, screaming in either pain or anger. Millie guessed the man was still in there somewhere, just as pathetic and evil.

# Chapter Eight

Experiment One

The next floor looked different than the most recent. It was cleaner, more sanitary, like it hadn't been attacked at all. The walls were full of reflections, reflections of themselves. Each door was cleaned with smooth precision, like someone had been living there, for years and years to come. But no one else had survived beside them, and Millie knew that.

"This is floor thirty-four. It holds documents about all the Experiments." Millie remembered, remembrance of everyone else, the others she failed to protect. 'Experiments,' she hated that word, hated it with every fiber of her being. But that was all they were called here, and everything they were ever going to be in the lab.

Silence remained by their side; no sounds were heard on the nasty floor above, nothing. Everything was cleaned and had somehow been preserved for all those years. It was like the place was still running, scientists roaming. The screams of kids in the back, screams of pain, worse than the ones of the monster above.

Charlie could hear it. She couldn't see them, but the echoes of it all remained to lurk in her head. The screams, the laughs of the insane, the orders, the money profiting. She could even hear the smiles, the *smiles* of pleasure, enjoyment of the pain, the money, the screams. She snapped back to reality, noticing everyone moving ahead, besides Millie.

"Are you okay, Charlie? You look upset," Millie asked, her voice deep with worry.

"I'm fine," Charlie mumbled, walking past Millie and towards the group. Millie stopped her though, stepping quickly in front of Charlie.

"Charlie, what's wrong?" Millie let out a loose breath. A different stare crossed Charlie's eyes, a stare of frustration.

"I'm fine," the girl sighed, nudging past her older friend.

Millie should have felt surprised at the anger held in Charlie's snap, but she wasn't, because she knew. Millie breathed in disappointment again, no words coming out that time. She didn't argue, didn't try and retort. There was no point. Charlie wasn't going to admit it. Some time she would, but not now. The two caught up with the rest, who seemed to not try and ask about what happened despite their curiosity, not mentioning a word of whatever that could've been.

The halls were full of the terror of even breathing and the silent footsteps of a bunch of kids. They could finally walk freely without having to worry about kicking their feet into rocks constantly. Millie let her finger run across the bandage, healing the bite mark.

The spotless halls were long, longer than the ones from the previous floors. The pure white color made the hall look like the entrance to heaven, disregarding the doors beforehand.

Charlie's green eyes glistened with the flickering lights swinging left and right above them. Her bleeding skin felt free from its pain; the bandages blocking it from exploding out of her wounds, but she knew that wouldn't last forever.

Millie had a sudden urge to explore some of the rooms. She stopped, twisting a doorknob, only for it to jam into something that locked it. Millie wasn't going to give up, her curiosity erupting inside of her. She slammed the door with her foot. Everyone stopped in their tracks, looking over at Millie in confusion. That thing had been screaming in pain for a while. So, it was probably still healing; she could make some noise at least, hopefully. Besides, a lot of doors have probably fallen in this place. She doubts it can tell the difference between a manually broken door or a cause of nature.

The door fell to the floor as the last kick hit. The room's walls were pure white as the halls. It looked like an office, including a desk, cabinets, and a coffee machine, as if completely untouched by the thing. Charlie joined Millie in her investigation as she wandered into the room, deciding to immediately snoop around as she saw the papers lying around on the desk.

Charlie yanked one off, putting it in a comfortable reading position. A document was what she held, with the words 'Experiment Twelve' written on the top as a title. It contained a bunch of information about the Experiment like, height, weight, age, gender, and then the ability, just like the rest of them. Millie decided to help with snooping, grabbing another paper on the table to read the contents of it.

"Experiment One," the title of Millie's paper said. She set it back down immediately, not caring for what information they had on her. She looked at Charlie's instead while she read it; it was more interesting to read about another one of the Experiments rather than herself.

Separation was something prioritized a lot in this facility. No one was allowed to see each other or socialize. All of them would have preferred school then this place. Charlie was surprised everyone had kept their social skills in the time they were stuck together. Millie wondered about the same question.

Charlie turned towards the back, planning to explore the room further. She noticed that some tapes were sitting behind them, begging to play. A video cassette recorder sat beside them, a tape already sticking out. In a place like a modern-day lab, she wasn't expecting them to have a video cassette recorder, but the place was known by employees for collecting and scavenging the new and old items. No one knew why, nor did the Experiments particularly care about how their own hell worked.

"Test zero, two." The cover title was scribbled, but it was clear enough to see. Millie watched as Charlie pushed the tape back into the recorder, backing up from the screen to get the whole view. Static rang into their ears before the video started. The sound felt far away, but they heard someone entering the room in the video.

The two girls were placed in the vision of a chair. A woman with tied back hair appeared, wearing what a scientist would, an experimenter. She looked down at the paper in her hands, opening her mouth to read it. Her face was barely visible in the blur the screen had, but they could live through it.

"Experiment One, our most powerful asset." She started on what would be a long video. Millie listened for the others outside. They were still there, waiting for them.

"Most information is unknown, but the most obvious is that the gender is female," the woman continued, tracing her finger across the page.

"She is the most strong, powerful, not like the others, being able to withstand more and more as we learn about her." She paused, along with a smile on her face. The reason was unknown.

"Experiment one can destroy anything in just a few seconds, metal, steel, or iron. Anything we throw, is gone with just the blink of an eye," the scientist explained, pointing a finger at what seemed like a blue eye.

"But she refuses to use them in some cases. In the battles of some experiments, she restricted herself from simply attacking. That means taking the beating from the other kid, which is least likely in most tests.

"Let's see her thoughts on the matter, shall we?"

The video blew into static, before all they saw was a chair, and they heard a door opening with a loud screech.

"Have a seat, please," a male voice was heard.

"Doctor Ratzfall," Millie grumbled, just as her figure sat in the swivel chair in the video.

"Experiment One. I'm going to ask you a few questions, and you are required to answer them."

Experiment One–Millie, nodded her head in agreement, resting her hands in her lap and staring directly into the camera. A high posture and annoyance plastered all over her face. Charlie has never seen this side of Millie before.

"Experiment One, do you have any clue where these powers had come from?" the first question asked, and soon to be the last.

Experiment One shook her head, muttering a "no" before going completely silent again.

"These powers are extraordinary. Being able to summon a weapon on your own is a useful trait, I must say," he said as a compliment.

"Why," was all Millie said, not a question, more like an opinion that needed to be shared.

He didn't have an answer for a second, only hesitating with the start of sentences, but they soon ended without any context.

"You…" he stuttered, he was shocked she was serious with it, "can summon a sword, Millie, do you realize how powerful you are? How much fear you have hatched among everyone else?"

"The only real reason I would need to summon a sword is self-defense." Millie's eyes could be felt from the heart in the video, like Charlie was Doctor Ratzfall himself.

"Do you think I am the type of person to feed on fear?" She stood up from her seat, leaning against the desk to stare him in the eyes.

"I don't care about power, and I can't believe you think that of me." Her fist went to the screen. Static screeched before black overtook white.

The video cut off then, the tape slithering out of the socket and falling to the floor. The two girls stood there for a moment. It was mostly Millie waiting for Charlie to say something, since she knew it was coming.

"Did you break the TV?" Charlie asked in shock, but a little snicker could be heard below it.

"Yeah," Millie sighed; she sounded disappointed that she did so.

"Wow, never thought of you as the type to..." her voice trailed off when she saw the annoyance on Millie's face at her own past mistakes. "Sorry, anyways..."

Charlie sauntered over to the other tapes, scrambling through multiple options of videos. Lisa peaked in, holding the door handle in her hands.

"What are you two doing?" Lisa asked, looking over at Charlie who was being nosy still. Then she stopped for a brief moment, noticing a busted cassette recorder that was cut in half.

"Searching through documents of other Experiments. Do you want to join us?" Millie offered, watching as Charlie examined another tape.

It said the numbers, 'Experiment Forty-Three' on the title. Charlie froze at the numbers. She placed one of her palms up, letting her see the small numbers that were cut into her palm and left as a scar to dry, and a reminder that her free will wasn't something she had anymore, not in this lab.

"Experiment, Forty-Three." The words still reminded her of the pain she felt that day, being taken to this place after the false accusations of her mother were set in stone. The screams she let out when they cut that in. It hurt, so bad, her head hurt just by the thought of it.

"That's about you, right?" Millie walked up beside Charlie, looking over Charlie's shoulder at the tape in the girl's hands.

Charlie nodded her head, never wanting to answer that question in any lifetime. Lisa fully opened the door, her eyes widening with realization and relation. She lifted her palm as well, 'Experiment Fifty-Six.'

She sighed, letting the hand fall to her side.

"We don't have to watch it—"

"You can. I'll go outside." Charlie handed the tape to Millie while she cut her off, holding it in the air until Millie took it from her fingers. She trudged out of the room, her legs feeling like paper again. The young girl closed the door behind them, not wanting to hear what they had to say about her. She didn't want to hear that story again, not when she was already struggling to forget about it.

Millie tossed the first tape aside yet hesitated to insert the second. Charlie had said they could but...

She placed it in, Lisa joining in this time. The same woman appeared, holding a piece of paper in her hands once more.

"Experiment Forty-Three, also known as Charlie Utinew, was here under the circumstances of a crime sequence in her family," she explained, a wicked smile spreading over her face.

"Her mother, Ellie Utinew, was accused of murdering her brother, Darlyn Utinew. She was sentenced to death by law, due to Matt Utinew, being the one who secretly committed the murder. He bribed the judge in exchange for ending Ellie's life, his own sister. Charlie was caught in all of this, but wasn't capable of speaking out after witnessing it, since Matt had filed for guardianship and eventually got permanent legal rights to keep her mouth always shut and a gun at her head."

Millie looked over at Lisa, whose eyes were filled with tears of pain for Charlie. Her mouth was covered by her hands.

"After a while though, the judge confessed, and Matt was sent to prison with a long sentence, but it didn't last for long when he was murdered by his cell inmate. Seems some don't take kindly to the abuse of children, especially not in jail."

"That's horrible…" she cried, her eyes steering over to Millie.

Millie had nothing to say. The case had been on thousands of screens across the world years ago, but hearing it again made her want to vomit for Charlie.

It explained a lot. It proved why Charlie had been so sacrificial. So willing to let her life be taken by the hands of death for everyone else. The girl thought she didn't deserve a life. Heartbreaking, just heart wrenching; Millie felt her heart shattering for Charlie. Everyone had known but hearing it in words was worse. It was terrible knowing that Charlie had lost her mother, who had been accused. Millie had seen a report at the lab once; this was just a reminder. Justice had been served too late, and now all that was left was the broken heart of a child, a lost and heartbroken girl. The tape had ended, but the two were too busy with pounding hearts for their friend. Charlie needed help, a lot of it, emotionally. She needed someone to hug, someone to understand her, someone she could cry with.

"I'll talk to her," Millie claimed, "want to come with?"

"You're...the best at that," Lisa said, "I might make it worse. Go talk to her."

The door opened, catching everyone's attention. Charlie sat the farthest away, her head resting in her own arms, and her arms alone.

Lisa exited first, giving Charlie a worried look as Millie walked out behind her, catching Charlie sitting in the back.

"Charlie. Can I talk to you alone, please?" Millie asked.

Charlie knew there wasn't a single reason she should say no. There wasn't a chance of protest, and words inside of her told her not to resist. Charlie got up and avoided accidentally pulling off the bandages.

Charlie followed Millie, who went further ahead, opening the nearest door. A bright light smashed her face as she let go of it, letting it slide by itself. Charlie ambled, meeting the light at the end. She stepped through the door, Millie following afterwards. As soon as the door shut, Millie started speaking to Charlie's despair.

"Charlie, you can't hide this anymore, or not much longer." Millie leaned on the door as she crossed her arms.

Charlie didn't say anything, knowing any argument would be easily countered.

"I know what happened, we both do now," Millie explained in her soft voice, starting to stride over to Charlie who didn't mutter a word against her. "I know that it seems like it was your fault, but trust me. None of that was in your control."

"We don't have time for this. I am fine." Charlie tried to make the argument stop, tried to end this conversation.

"Charlie, you are shaking." Millie was right; she was. "We have plenty of time right now. It's been screaming for ages; it should take a while to heal a gouged-out eye."

*Why was she doing this?*

"You don't know exactly when it will get back up!" Charlie snapped, feeling something inside of her. Something snapped, something large, causing Millie to jump back, but barely, her eyes widening with shock and concern.

What did she just say? What did she just do? What had she *done?*

"I'm sorry, I–I didn't mean that."

She started rocking back and forth. She didn't know why, maybe it was some way to calm herself down? Well, it certainly wasn't working. Millie seemed to notice, unlike how Charlie didn't notice herself, didn't recognize herself, didn't even know herself. What was she? A child? A girl? A monster? What was she anymore after everything that had happened? Who even was she? Questions floated in her head, questions she wished for answers for, and at the same time, wanted them to disappear. She felt herself floating into a flurry of blur, hearing a ring in her ear, a sign? A sign of what? Her own insanity?

"Charlie?"

A voice was heard in the sea of her own screams; of her own misery she was still hiding. Her own insanity.

"Charlie. Are you okay?" She couldn't breathe, why couldn't she breathe? She yelled at herself to breathe, just open her mouth and breathe, but she couldn't.

The voice had come back again. It wasn't leaving her alone. A mist lay ahead of her, a mist of lies. A mist of a lie that she was told by everyone around her. She wasn't a girl. She wasn't Charlie. She was a monster—

A figure lay ahead in the fog. A familiar figure. A figure with such bright blue eyes stared at her, but she couldn't tell what emotion they wielded against her without the rest of the face. The young girl couldn't tell.

"Charlie. Wake up, please."

She snapped back to reality in a quick open of her eyes; she saw Millie standing in front of her, holding a hand on Charlie's shoulder, which was full of her own sweat. No words escaped her mouth; she kept silent, lowering her head.

"Charlie, guilt hurts, it always does. I go through the same thing every day." Those last words shocked Charlie like thunder. What did Millie have to be guilty about?

"I feel guilty for..." she paused, "for not saving them, the others in the lab on time."

Millie fought to keep her tears in, but she did so anyway. "It hurts every day, and I know it hurts for you, but hiding it doesn't help, for neither of us."

Millie had said it sometimes, but it seemed she kept it to herself mostly to not upset the others all the time. Her friend took a step back.

Charlie felt her words roaming inside her heart, but the tears still wouldn't come.

"You don't deserve to die, Charlie." Millie sighed. "We can get through this, together. Please?"

Millie raised her arms out, offering a hug that they both really needed. She didn't expect Charlie to run into it right away, but her friend killed her expectations and rammed herself into Millie's arms.

The tears streamed down Millie's shoulder; her crying was silent still. Someone who didn't want to be heard.

"Just let it out. You don't have to do this alone anymore," Millie cried, feeling her own tears escape along with her friends.

The pain had always haunted her ever since her mother's death. The tears that she held so silently were always taunting her, mocking her constantly inside of her head.

No tears were left either, coming down like a river; that was exactly how she felt. Millie's shoulder was now full of water and tears. It continued down her gown and vanished into the white dress, nowhere to be seen, ever again. It was an amazing feeling to recognize that someone knew, for someone to understand her; she was free from the silence. Free from all of it, like it had vanished, felt like it had never been there at all. She was free, free from the quiet look that people gave, free from it all.

"Promise me one thing, alright?" asked Charlie. "No more trying to sacrifice yourself as a distraction, and I won't either."

"Deal."

A small smile went across Charlie's face, free, finally free. But it was never that easy, and she knew that, but someone finally understood her through this madness. Someone to assure her that it would be okay, and that she was safe from him, that murderer. Millie was thinking the same thing as Charlie, but she was not alone. The ordeal Charlie had gone through was terrible, an example of how cruel the world could be, but Millie would help her get through it, help all of them get through it...this, their friends, to fight through this tragedy, and what might be freedom.

# Chapter Nine

An Evil Guard

The group fled the area slowly. The monster hadn't attacked them, that meant something was bound to happen. Silence was never a good thing in these types of scenarios. It twisted a weird feeling, one of fear and terror of what was to come. Little noise surrounded them, not inside of Charlie, only fear shouted at her now.

The light of the hall swirled around with the spinning lights overhead, moving with the group as they strolled down, relieved that they didn't have to worry about tripping on rubble. Charlie breathed heavily, despite trying her best to keep it quiet. It left her with a hoarse and loud sound; she eventually gave up stopping it since no one seemed to mind. Exhaustion fell down her legs; her feet were barely able to keep up with her friends, wobbling with every step, shaking with every breath. Her eyes were about to close on her, but she had to keep moving. The kids had stopped ten times before; she couldn't be the reason it moved up to eleven.

The glow of the man-made lights flickered like fireflies around them, the luxurious brightness blinding anything that came near, as a siren led its victims to death. Except this wasn't the sense of death, the lights wouldn't cause it at least.

The monster remained quiet; a roar or a growl hadn't been heard from it in a while. Maybe it was, and they just couldn't hear it, meaning they were far enough. They had been gifted a break. An incredibly long one, thanks to Millie.

Charlie activated her ability, the walls becoming translucent, beckoning to her eyes will. It took her a while to spot the generator, which stood on the far side of the floor. In a corner, patiently waiting.

"Over there," Charlie muttered quietly, pointing towards the box through the walls.

The kids followed along with Charlie's statement, peeking over every corner, searching through all the stone walls. The generator felt so far away, as if the whole world was in their way.

A ring went into Millie's ear, a warning. She whipped her head around down the hall they had been walking through. Silence trailed them, chasing them until it reached their bodies.

Her journey down the hall had stopped; everyone looked at her in suspicion, not at her but what was to come. Charlie noticed her suspicion, so she looked up slowly, only to see the figure right above them once it was revealed to her.

Charlie was only able to take a step back right as the ceiling broke over her head, targeting her exact position. It seemed like this thing hated her now, for constantly stopping it from reaching the others.

Millie tackled Charlie out of the way faster than the monster could thrash a claw, slamming them both into the wall.

Mitchell got slashed by the frantic weapon as soon as it landed, blood now leaking from the scratch on his face. The monster grinned, standing before Mitchell as it grabbed his throat and lifted him into the air. Millie picked up some random rock off the ground from the crash. She leaped from the floor, clenching the rock in her fingers, but was only able to get a few feet to its head before it caught her by the throat, stopping her intervention.

Lisa tried to help, yet one swipe from its claw sent her flying at least ten feet down the hallway. Michael tried something as well, whipping a rock at its head. The monster ducked, letting the rock fall beside it, knowing that it would cause little damage, but dodged it just to show him that his attack was pointless, useless, that he was *useless*. They couldn't do anything, couldn't help, all they could do was wait until what happened next, unfortunately that remained to be the monster's choice. Charlie didn't know what to do either in her newfound spot. She could only watch in fear and horror as two friends were about to be slashed with the scythe of death.

A spike of some light went through Mitchell's body, grabbing everyone's attention. Another emerged, electric bolts surrounding his skin, running through his body like a sentient being that knew what it was doing.

Charlie realized he was touching an electrical wire next to him that was hanging from an electrical box. Was he absorbing it? Was it normal? She couldn't tell. The wire sparked with lights, going directly into Mitchell's arm, and into his system, countless following afterwards. He noticed the traveling and immediately removed his arm from the wire, but it was too late, and the electricity exploded. A scream erupting loudly from his mouth as blue light streamed around his figure, soaring in yellow and white and a shrivel of pain throughout his body.

The bolts zoomed to the nearest candidate, the monster. It let out a monstrous roar as the electricity spread across its skin, burning it alive in blazes of pain as it dropped Millie to the ground; the electricity didn't get a chance to go for her next.

"Run!" she shouted, galloping into a full run as she scrambled onto her two feet.

The monster fought through the pain of being electrocuted, screaming in pain as the lightning attacked it, flying across its black skin and flaming it like it was on the roof of the sun. Mitchell's body was still smoking from the heat, like a gun after being fired. His body turned numb with the stomach cramping that pushed him down. Mitchell's legs fainted, pulling him down onto the floor, but he felt Millie's hand grab his arm as she pulled him alongside her.

They couldn't hide, their only chance of survival now was sprinting away, and fighting. Hiding was something they wished they could do, but it wasn't tricking them anymore. The children knew it could see through the walls. There would be no point in doing that now, not when the kids knew the truth.

The group bolted towards the generator, forgetting to realize it would be a horrible idea to lead the monster directly to it, directly to their source of freedom. It wasn't stupid to recognize how each elevator was able to work after all that time.

The sounds of the kids' breathing, footsteps, and even their quiet fear were heard as they fled down the halls, to the generator, and to their secret plan against the monster that it was soon to understand.

Charlie peeked her eyes over her shoulder, checking their backs only to see black claws crush the corridor. The head poking out with white eyes stared directly back. She turned her head back forward out of horror, keeping her focus on the path ahead. The path of life instead of the wide road of death.

Her legs had no time to even think of exhaustion. Time is delicate now, fragile. She had to use it wisely. Each decision could decide the future; each decision was as important as the sun in the solar system. Her shoulders ached from the constant movement from left to right. She ignored their pleas to stop, her feet continuing to run across the ground, sliding over stone a little, but not enough to trip fortunately.

Millie scanned their surroundings, looking for some sort of weapon to defend them, to defend her friends, her *family*. She could hold it off long enough for Michael to fix the generator. Charlie felt the fear punching her guts, like they were about to pop, burst and spill all her energy inside of her until it escaped through the breaths of her mouth.

Her bandages held tightly. She was somehow able to run despite being on the verge of falling earlier. Her teeth chattered, barely being able to control themselves with the amount of fear climbing inside of her. They were almost there, almost to the generator. They were close, so close. Millie rounded a corner. Michael followed right behind her, along with the others.

*So close, almost there.* Charlie kept repeating those words in her head, words that she should've used a while ago, but at the same time she recognized they wouldn't have helped then. The wind slapped them in the face, like it was shouting at them to move faster. Keep going, just keep going, keep pushing through the pain in their legs, their bodies and minds. Their running didn't stop at all, their legs sprinting towards the generator with everything they had. The group was at least seven feet away. Charlie looked back again, only to see nothing, just air, the doors, the hall, but not the monster. No claw marks were on the floor from the monster running on all fours, like they had been running from nothing at all, like the beast had been only a fragment of their imagination.

The ceiling exploded in front of Millie, splattering halls of stone right at her head. The monster landed on its feet, menacingly raising its head and looming over her with its eyes glowing brighter as the head faced her. It blocked the door to the generator, their only way to enter the next floor. The group backed up in a panic, freezing in their terror just by the sight of it. Millie picked up a rock; it would do little damage, but it was something. Silence surrounded them, crawling into the wind that blew from nowhere, something they wanted to see, but had no chance to do so.

Millie threw the stone at the head, missing the eye by an inch, but it didn't move from its position. The girl highly expected it to lunge at her out of anger, but it didn't even plan on attacking. That's when it clicked in Charlie's head. It was blocking them; it had figured it out. It was guarding the generator. It knew that it was their only way out of this, and it stopped them from reaching their chance.

"You got to be kidding..." Lisa mumbled with a low voice, watching Millie search around for some kind of fatal weapon.

Mitchell looked around for any electrical wires next to them. There was nothing, nothing he could do to help, just plain old stone walls with rocks that lay underneath. How were they supposed to get past this?

Another rock hit the monster in the chest, but it still didn't move. It wasn't going to get distracted by anything. Millie guessed this definitely took a lot of restraint for it.

"Hey, you had no other option, so you decided to be a puppy guard. How pathetic," Lisa insulted suddenly, moving to the right of the monster.

It kept its gaze on her, the glowing eyes meeting hers as it let out a snarl of anger. She started shaking, those eyes felt like she was staring into the orbs of death itself, but she continued her snarky smile as she waved her arms around. Everyone stared at her in confusion, but soon they noticed Michael creeping to the left, trying to get past the monster and into the door with a wrench.

The monster felt his presence, immediately whooping around and raising its arm to strike, swinging as Michael jumped back by Millie who was about to knock it in the head. He squirmed back by the group; Lisa gained her original position as well. One plan eliminated; less ideas were revealed in the group's brains. How was this supposed to go? What were they supposed to do? That thing would kill anyone who tried to get past, like a gatekeeper guarding a kingdom. A king who played with the only subjects left under his control.

The teeth were showing, the white fangs full of some of their dried blood, mostly Charlie's and Millie's. Millie thought of tackling it again, but there was a chance she would push it into the room behind, giving them no other way to progress. She had a sudden sting in her arm, making her clench it. She took a moment to examine her arm, keeping an eye on the monster that stared at her in disgust. Millie gave a snarling stare right back. That didn't work on her; it never did. She tried to call out to her Lord in her head and tried to ask what to do next. What did He want her to do? There was simply silence, but words were felt, so she waited, waited for another to have a go.

The standoff lasted for a while, each side waiting for the other to make a move. The kids mostly thought of some way to get past it, but less options showed up to the party of their minds. The ones that did show themselves had some bad attribute that canceled it out immediately, eliminating it to the point of no use at all. The monster was still, not a single movement from it, not even an inch. Breathing was even something that it refused to do sometimes, as if it was useless. Charlie was praying in her head for it to pass out of its own stupidity. A growl or snarl would come out of its mouth every time the kids subtly stepped closer.

Millie met its glare, as if it saw what she was thinking, saw the thoughts and consideration of the use of the power in her body. It pounded at her, screamed and begged to be let out, to take over the weak and small soul that was too weak to handle it. It was a blade to her head; it pleaded, begged. It wanted out.

*Out, out, out.* Now.

No.

This thing wasn't planning on moving. It would never move, not even for a second was it going to leave its spot. Its claws were full of dried-up cold blood, from the bodies of tiny children, but it didn't matter. Not for a second would it have even a slice of sympathy for the brats that stood in its way. Kids who just wanted to go home, kids who wanted their lives back.

The group wasn't going to give up, especially if they had come this far, now was not the time, not when they were so close to catching freedom. Silence was screams to their ears between the few feet in the middle of Millie and the monster, between the flesh craving beast and the group.

The floor had gone quiet; the rats only squeaking once in a few minutes, but other than that, nothing. It started moving side to side, facing its head in the direction of the kids. It was getting impatient; it wanted fun, to relieve itself of its boredom. Confidence, that was something they could use to their advantage against it. Millie recalled all thoughts of this thing, then others around her. She didn't know why, but a thought was telling her. The thought turned into someone.

Millie glanced at Lisa, who was wondering what solution they could have for this problem, keeping her eyes on the beast without even blinking. Lisa looked over at Millie after finishing her pondering, sensing her friend's dark blue eyes. Charlie noticed their silent conversation, looking back and forth between the two. Millie raised a finger, pointing it to her own eye.

Lisa didn't catch on immediately, having to peek at the monster occasionally to remember, but then she understood, knew what she needed to. Charlie raised an eyebrow, wondering what the heck the two had conjured up with no words at all. Lisa turned her attention to her brother, who was staring at the monster in case it decided to lunge.

Only out of pure fear did he stare at it, because when it was gone, that was when it turned bad, dang bad.

He sensed his sister's eyes; his brow also raised in confusion as she stared at him. She pointed to the wrench he had been holding for a while, making sure the monster was not looking. If it was smart enough to realize what they were planning, it could definitely recognize their silent talk. He looked down at the wrench, putting the pieces together on what he was assigned to do. Same plan as before, just a different distraction.

Lisa then raised a finger towards her eye, signaling what her part of the assignment was. Michael responded with a nod; the pieces finally connected. Lisa prepared herself as she faced the monster, her eyes threatening something it didn't know about.

In a quick glance, Lisa bolted.

"Cover your eyes!" Millie's hands went over Sally's before the girl could realize what was happening.

Lisa's eyes glowed white as the flash brightened, covering the whole room in a bright piercing fog. They heard the monster scream through their ears, covering their eyes to avoid the light that would have surely caused intense pain. Michael made his move, still squeezing his eyes shut as he felt a touch of the monster's skin when he slid past and rammed the door. His hand frantically searched for the doorknob, finding it in a matter of moments before he slipped inside and shut himself in. Michael paced his eyes around, finding the generator at the back of the room. The wrench was through the hole immediately, whipping around, hitting everything, making slight sparks in the darkness that ended with a clank. It felt like forever as he did it, like the time in the safe room all over again.

Something fell to the ground as he hit one last time, the generator clicking on again like a flashlight with the impact. He plucked himself out of the hole that all the generators conveniently had, like they had been there just for them, like someone had punched them through the machines for this exact moment. Just for them, like a present on Christmas Day. It had been just for them, or some miracle had been brought into their lives. It could have been anything, but all he knew was that he was grateful, grateful for life.

He turned back towards the door that was shielding him from the light, slowly taking some steps to get closer to it, hearing for any commotion on the other side. How long had he been in that generator?

It felt fast, but at the same time it took forever for him to flick it on. He took one last step until he was right in front of the gate. He heard nothing but the silence of the wind. That was what this whole place was, silence, pure quiet, the complete opposite of what it had been before. All he heard were the screams of young people, the laughs of the wicked, and the money slipping into their hands. That's all his brain remembered, and he always wished it didn't. The door slowly glided across the floor as he opened it, a light slamming him in the face. It wasn't the one from his sisters though, just regular. The one they had been walking under for hours at least, or days even. He didn't see anyone. They had vanished, vanished into what no human being on earth could comprehend.

"Hello—"

The words didn't have time to leave his mouth before Millie tackled him. The monster lunged into the door he had just exited straight afterwards, missing him by a second. It seemed he hadn't paid much attention to the hall in front of him.

"Cover your eyes!" Millie ordered for the second time, covering her own as Lisa surprised the monster.

The world erupted into what looked like the gates of heaven once again. The monster screamed in pain as it had done before; the eyes too bright for its own to handle for even a second. It didn't learn from the last time; its anger was too much for that slim body to handle, despite conjuring it up for so long.

A sting of exhaustion fled through her bare legs. Lisa felt like she was about to collapse, but she kept her eyes open and stood her ground. Once the light had faded, the group had left before the monster had a slight chance to stop one of them. The pain in its face was too intense for it to do anything at that moment, all because of that frustration and desire that drives it forward, but down to the floor.

The kids ran back the way they came; Millie somehow being able to remember the exact coordinates of their path. The elevator was soon found again, everyone jamming themselves into the lift while the doors were still opening. Patience was not on their side, nor their minds. No one wanted to stick around just to see that thing chase after them again. The children felt relieved; they had escaped to another floor after a close call, again.

Then the screech came, and the peace that had once soothed through their heads was left behind. They all turned to the hallway, seeing the monster stumble to the ground on all fours like a rabid animal, quickly lifting itself to its feet. The eyes of a beast staring at the kids with such anger that it sent a gulp down Charlie's throat.

It bolted, kicking rocks that its feet landed on every step of the way. Screaming in absolute anger and frustration, it wasn't finished, and it wasn't going to just let them go again. The elevator wouldn't close on time; the doors were slower than usual, like fate had suddenly betrayed them, turning its back on them for good. Michael anxiously pressed the button that should have closed the doors faster, yet he knew it wouldn't work. The monster roared as it reached twenty feet away from the door, pleasure exciting its voice as it saw the kids' frightened faces. Even the tall brat that had almost murdered it, who was placing herself in front of everyone, eyes widened with horror as she pressed her lips with the stupid courage she's always had.

It transitioned to its two feet, raising a claw as it leaped through the air with the wind whipping around it as fast as a tornado, a hurricane of terror.

The intensity of the situation stopped; it landed in front of them but didn't go any further than the elevator door. The monster towered over them, as if the menace inside the beast would make them drop right then and there. It stared through Millie's concentrated eyes. Something had stopped it; it couldn't have been the glare from Millie. They had done that for at least fifteen minutes, and it hadn't even considered backing down once.

The group watched as the angered stare of the monster was soon shut out once the doors closed. Millie's hand tightened, blocking something out of the view of the kids, something hidden. Deep within her, not given by the world nor received.

# Chapter Ten
### Failed Lives

The doors slid open, revealing the next level of the game. The game between life and death that they had won so many times, but fate could overtake them, resulting in losing. Losing was not a good option in the circumstances they were in.

*Floor thirty three.*

Millie stepped out first as usual, scanning the area. Something felt wrong at that moment. She knew what it was; the monster wasn't on the floor yet; they would have heard it then. It was the generator, there was something wrong about it.

Charlie searched the floor, not seeing the monster in her sight. She couldn't find the generator yet due to the mess the floor had become, or had been for such a long time, and it had started so many years ago.

She watched as Millie stepped forward, her body moving so fluidly that it looked like water as her foot kicked a large rock out of the way. The floor was like the rest, abused by the power and beauty of the natural world, compared to the lab's decay and rot. It had started to take this floor; vines were growing from the ceiling and on the stone walls, only being able to tickle their hair follicles. Charlie followed after Millie, the rest of the group already behind her lead.

She raised her arm back at the vines, letting them tangle around her arm as she walked along with the group, sending a cold signal through her skin, cold like the snow on the first day of December. What day was it anyways? How long had it even been? It felt like years, but she didn't know that for sure. It could have been, considering how much food they had survived off of. That safe room had it all, but it wouldn't have lasted them forever. It felt like forever, the same routine every morning, and every night. It felt like the days of school, a school she so desperately longed for. She remembered back before it all happened, before she was brought here. Specific children hated school, and wished to skip the entire school years, but for Charlie.

That was something she wanted to go to one day, school. Where she could make more friends, meet new people, learn something new in life, and she hoped the same for the rest of them. She at least wanted to see it, see the sky once in life before her body shut down on her. Before her last breath, just once would she want to see outside, just once. Charlie thought about that as they crept towards the generator. She was giving them directions occasionally to tell them where to go, but before that. It was just the thought of outside, everything out there was beautiful, and she wanted to see it, hear it, smell it, touch it. All her senses craved to see outside, and she hoped that those cravings would be fulfilled, and the vines were one of them. She realized that now, those were from outside, and she had touched it. One touch, one, then it turned to two as she continued, raising her fingers towards the vines until they could at least hit the tip. She hoped this wish could come true, for all of them.

She didn't want to die, not here.

Her patched skin, covered in rotting bandages that needed to be removed and replaced. *Removed*, that was one word to describe her, removed from her family, removed from life itself. Had life hated her? Was that why it was so messed up? Her emotions hadn't helped that much. Letting all the tears contained inside of her like a jar. They had been released, but the depression didn't follow along. It stayed, just to torment her, reminding her of that thing she regretted so much. But it wasn't anything, because she blamed herself, no one else but her. She knew it wouldn't help that much, to cry until she couldn't anymore, until her stomach wanted to throw up, but it felt good to do so, felt good to know someone understood. Someone knew what she was going through, and people she could relate to, a group that could help each other. She was only a child, a mere child who could do nothing in the face of the law. The only thing she did was hope, but that hadn't done anything. Due to that, her mother was killed, killed for something that didn't have anything to do with her, something she had no knowledge about. Then the government whisked her off, forcing her through such pain that she felt she had no capability of reacting. They were used to it. Her eyes had turned dull, lost of all the twinkles of light that had fought for so long to brighten, but that effort had no effect, and all she could do was take it until her last breath escaped.

She hadn't realized they had made it to the generator. Charlie had been so caught up in her own memories that burned her alive that she hadn't realized the huge problem they were facing. The generator stood there, chipped gears scattered across the floor, no longer usable, along with no way to fix them. The generator was barely a generator anymore. The batteries were gone; the wires had been cut or damaged during the attack. This floor must've had some strong fighters, because whoever was in here had put up a fight.

Charlie realized as Millie walked over to a corner, that the person was still there. A skeleton, still fully intact, but with no soul. The monster possibly kept the person alive with some sort of power while it tortured them. Either that, or it knew exactly where to bite to put the most pain into the person without killing them. What cruel tactics to learn for the sick desires of pain and torment. All Mille could do was make out that it was a boy. The eyes filled with nothing but pure darkness and emptiness. A red river that was now solid had been pouring down, ending at the neck. The rib cage of the chest was gone, so his stomach had been ripped out. His torso sat empty; blood dried along his bones.

The boy sat in a corner, sitting quietly with his soul gone. The hands were laid gently down on the knees, like he had given up at some point, and simply accepted the painful fate that awaited him. Dark red shot eye sockets stared at Millie as she stood close to the corpse, stepping by the giant stains of blood on the ground. Sally kept her eyes away, but took a few glances, unable to even think of what that was while holding on tightly to Lisa, who kept the curious kid's head away.

"Experiment Twelve," Millie muttered, picking up the hand as she grimaced. She recognized him just by the bones.

It was impressive but also confusing to Charlie. It was the same kid from the document they had found earlier, poor boy. Millie felt the memory returning to kill her, like a vengeful ghost coming after the murderer. She couldn't save anyone else. The only ones surviving were the kids standing behind her, waiting to finally free themselves from this forgotten dump that had no meaning anymore. If it did, then they would have been moved to some other lab, where the tests went on and on, until the kids couldn't take it anymore. Unless the government believed there were no survivors in the massacre. Millie raised the hand, pressing the red fingertips against her forehead, showing respect, respect for the dead, for this boy that lost his life so brutally and painfully, and she prayed that up in the sky. He was safe, smiling, and happy.

She released it, letting it fall like a feather onto his lap again. No one questioned why she did it, or how 'disgusting' it was. Even if he was long gone, he never deserved to be forgotten, erased from memories. Nor did he deserve what happened to him. Lisa doubted he had been forgotten by those he knew.

They were barely able to focus their attention back onto the generator, which was in shambles. Nothing left but the scraps of the catastrophe.

"What am I supposed to do with this?" Michael said, his voice was shaky and unrecognizable.

"There's nothing you can do, Micheal. We will have to find another way," Millie claimed somehow calmly, the scent of the empty body finally kicking in.

The screams of the boy that day, before his tongue had been ripped from his body, eliminating his ability to speak. Pain, that's all he had experienced before his end, awful, horrible. It wanted to see him cry, see him gurgle in pain as it tore out his throat.

She couldn't erase that thought from her head. Her thoughts, her mind, showed her what she had left. What she left to die so painfully. She felt the eyes of the other children staring at her. She had protected them, and no one else. Millie had a hand placed to her head, pinching her skin like it would erase the memory, but she couldn't escape it; no one would ever be able to.

"Let's go," Millie said, her voice full of guilt. Every thought went into her mind to taunt her, taunt her of her past mistakes. That one mistake had left everyone around her scarred. The people she had forgotten, the people she had betrayed.

"Millie?"

The voice snapped her back to reality, and when it did, she realized tears were rolling down her face, and everyone could see it.

"I'm sorry." How stupid was she? She was supposed to be strong, to not let them down, to not let them be afraid.

"What's wrong?" Charlie asked, stepping forth from the group.

Millie only stared at Charlie, then her eyes darted away, staring at the door, only to close it a moment later to try and pull back the tears that kept coming. A raspy breath was sucked back into her throat, as if trying to calm herself, to try and get rid of them.

"Millie," Charlie spoke again; her voice was sincere, guess the roles had been reversed this time.

"It's…" Millie wanted to say 'nothing,' her mind begged her to be rid of this, but…they promised to help each other, didn't they?

"It's just…" Millie started, but she was barely able to get herself to finish. "All of them. They…died, because…" Her words didn't want to finish the sentence. "I couldn't save them. I was able to save you all, but they…they were left to die. I…left them to…"

"Millie…they died because the monster killed them. You tried your best, and you did good. What else were you supposed to do during that?" Michael butted in.

"Yeah, we are all kids," Lisa continued, stopping herself just an inch ahead of Charlie.

Charlie stepped forward and embraced herself around Millie as she said, "My problem or any of ours doesn't make it any less important. The monster isn't here anyways."

Millie broke down right then and there, wrapping her arms around her friend as she silently cried into the hug. Lisa joined in, finding a spot by Millie's side. Michael came after, along with the other two.

"You did your best," Charlie muttered, over Millie's cries and tears.


Millie was silent as the group trotted back towards the elevator. Michael had suggested seeing if they could fix something in the elevator to get it going, but they didn't know for sure if that was true though. They could only hope, have faith and pray that they would be saved from this place, or they would be left to die in their sorrow and insanity of this stone cave. The walls felt like they were closing in on them; no one else seemed to notice it but Charlie.

Charlie felt butterflies ramming into each side of her stomach. Her stress filled her with an overwhelming feeling of pain from that thing. After she saw what that boy had gone through, before death. She didn't want to feel that as her final thought, and she knew everyone else felt the same.

The rubble around them danced as they kicked them out of the way, tumbling into walls, or simply stopping in its tracks. A lone rock, sitting on an abandoned building, left to sit still for eternity. The same way the kids had felt each day they had been stuck in that safe room. It was safe, but it didn't keep them free from their torment of loneliness and isolation.

The elevator was seen down the hall once again, sitting silently, unable to do its job anymore. Michael went ahead, scanning the machine for any problems with it. It only ran on the generators on each floor, but there had to be some way to get it running, some way to get it to move again. To do its job one last time before the last human survivors left this place for good. The area went silent as Michael investigated the elevator, too quiet. Charlie had felt it, felt the slam of the quiet hall straight in her stomach. She looked over at Millie, whose eyes darted around them; she obviously felt the same way. Something large was engraved in Charlie's head, a feeling. The same thing Millie had always talked about when she felt it. It was before danger happened, and that got Charlie to whip around just in time before a claw went straight through her stomach. Blood recoiled into the air, as some wept from her mouth.

"Charlie!" Millie screamed her name, grabbing the claw of the monster as it slashed for her face. She held it tightly, somehow being able to hold off the strength of the experiment.

"Run! Get in the elevator!" Millie ordered, stopping the second attack that almost could've clawed her eye out.

Lisa yanked Charlie's limp body off the ground and into her arms, cramming in the elevator last. Millie heard the doors slowly closing. She heard the gurgle of blood leaving Charlie's cough. The blood was pouring down her stomach. She was dying, right when she could achieve her dream. No, no, no...please God.

She punted the monster off her, giving her just enough time to reach the elevator. Millie whipped around, bolting as fast as her strength could carry her towards those already closing doors. They showed her reflection staring right back at her with anxious eyes, terrified as the monster lunged for her.

She leaped, squeezing through in time before the doors shut her out.

She saw Charlie in the corner, almost dead, sitting as Experiment Twelve did. Charlie reached out her hand to her, and they locked together for Millie's healing power to work.

A drop was heard, almost slamming Sally into the ground, then Millie remembered. The elevator hadn't been fixed, at all.

The elevator shook again before starting its fall.

The lights flickered rapidly as the elevator went into a nosedive like an airplane, plummeting towards God knew where. Everyone held onto each other, holding tightly in case this was their last chance to.

Charlie hugged Lisa and Millie together, hiding her face in whoever's shoulder she was closest to. Wind passed through them, almost flinging them into the roof. Their legs held strong on the floor, as a breeze like a hurricane dashed through them left and right, swinging them around like dolls, like the tiny children they were, but had little chance to be.

Then a slam shook the elevator. They all flew into the roof no matter how hard they held onto whatever they had found, and every single one of them crashed to the floor. Charlie landed on top of Millie and then rolled off to the side. The oldest had done that purposely, to protect her from the fall. She already had a hole in her stomach; broken bones were the last thing she needed. Charlie had opened her eyes fully due to the crash; the pain from the hole in her stomach evaporating into nothing.

The hole was still there, but her vision wasn't blurring anymore; the blood had stopped escaping. She could see clearly; her head wasn't pounding like her rapid heartbeat. Charlie felt nothing, nothing but the wind stampeding through the elevator one last time. Not even the dizziness of the wound was affecting her. The fall had been quick; how far had they dropped?

Millie got to her feet, turning to Charlie who was clutching onto her stomach like she was trying to keep the blood out, but it didn't escape in a conquest any further.

"Is everyone okay?" Millie asked around, no one said the word 'no.'

The hole hadn't been too large, so they were able to bandage it well with a medkit they had found on the next floor, only to keep Charlie comfortable since no one wanted to walk around with an open claw wound in their chest. The floor was just like the rest, torn to bits until all that was left was the walls and floors that could only hold strong for so long.

# Chapter Eleven
Sally's Sleep

As the group walked, Sally felt as if her legs were about to collapse on her. She didn't try to say anything, a strong pulse inside of her heart and mind told her to say something, so they could stop and rest, but no. If they stopped again, then it would take longer and longer for them to make it to the exit. She couldn't say something, she couldn't—

Sally swayed onto her side, collapsing into the ground with a shaking body. She could hear everyone's feet come to a halt as she lifted herself to her knees, where they rapidly vibrated with sore muscles as they attempted to keep her small, weak body upright.

"Sally? What's wrong?" Millie's voice was the first to respond to her situation at that moment.

Sally shook her head in response, but slowly did it go. She pushed herself until she was standing on her feet, but she was shaky. It felt like her hands were about to fall off her arms if she even tried to move them. Millie wasn't that far away, only staring at Sally from afar. She soon took another step closer, speaking her name again in a more soft and gentle voice, yet it felt so far away, so…

Millie was able to rush over in time as Sally lost her balance, falling into her arms as her eyes closed into dark unconsciousness.

"Is she okay?" Lisa asked in a worried tone, putting her hands to her mouth in shock as she stepped forward in front of the others.

"Yeah...she's okay, just tired," Millie explained, carrying Sally in her arms. "Remember how I said my powers would kill me if I used them?"

The group nodded their heads.

"It's the same for everyone; except you all will only pass out from exhaustion. It depends on how advanced the power is." Millie stared down at Sally with a concerned look.

A loud bang hit the kids like a train, startling them. The group searched the area, huddling together like animals against a threat.

"Above," Charlie whispered.

A crack came from ahead of them, rocks falling to the floor and tumbling around. Shaking arrived next, almost knocking Mitchell over, but Michael pulled him back to his feet before he knocked himself out next. The shake swung left and right, and the roof splattered, revealing the monster's tall thin body, the claws that caused so much bloodshed, that caused mass slaughter of man were ready by its sides.

"Run!" Millie screamed, no hesitation in her sprint towards the children.

Lisa got everyone to move before the monster reached them, each one of them exhausted, tired, but they didn't fall or falter. They kept bolting.

All the wounds she had gained pulled her down, pulled her into the deepest pits of fire, but Charlie climbed back out as her feet jumped smoothly through all the cobble beneath her. It hurt but now could never be the time to worry about her discomfort.

The wounds burned with even the tiniest inch of movement. It made her want to cry, cry until this place was full of her own tears of blood and sorrow, but all she could do now was hope and pray for somewhere where they could all finally rest. Rest soundly with no fear tormenting them, but soon, she saw it.

A safe room, far away from them, locked behind a metal door just down the hall.

"Safe room!" Charlie yelled; those were the only words she could say.

The monster picked up its pace, galloping on all fours like the beast it was, the beast it had always been inside, and only decided to improve.

Millie was able to get there first, still holding Sally in her arms as she yanked the door open. She waited by the door anxiously as everyone else jumped in, handing Sally to Lisa who didn't hesitate. She slid inside last, seeing the monster a few feet away from the door.

The metal door slammed, sending an echo across the floor. Millie held onto the knob for a moment as it roared on the other side. A bang wailed, hitting the door viciously, shaking the whole entire room with its screams of anger, then another hit and another. Again, and again.

None of them wanted to move at all, in case that door flew off its hinges. Millie ignored it unlike the rest of them; she trotted over to a couch and took Sally from Lisa on the way, muttering a thank you as she laid Sally gently on the cushions.

"She just needs some rest." Millie slowly strolled to the bedrooms. The oldest disappeared into the darkness of the hallway.

The group stood there in silence, some of them still flinched at the banging on the door. A roar as loud as a lion followed afterwards. They couldn't do anything with that thing hitting the door like a train, but they would have to get used to it until Sally woke up. So, the group went off to do their own things. Each one of them hoped the monster would get tired soon.

It wouldn't stop, no matter how many minutes passed by it wouldn't stop. It slammed on the door constantly, banging and roaring loudly in anger. The built-up rage over the past few hours the kids had been running from it had somehow increased its ability to do more, to not even consider its actions. No action it did would it ever regret. It resembled the man it once was, greedy, selfish, taking pleasure in hurting others. That would never leave it, even if it transformed into what it was today.

Lisa stood in front of the door, so used to the banging that she wasn't scared anymore. She was...just annoyed, like the rest of them. She crossed her arms like an annoyed mother who was waiting at the door for her son to come home after sneaking out. That's something she used to do with Michael before their life took a turn into a horrifying chapter. She tapped her foot, like the monster would hear it. Lisa let out a long sigh, praying that the experiment would stop. She watched as Charlie paced back and forth behind her, taking a few glances at Sally who was still cuddled into a dream. If she was even dreaming, whatever she was thinking. Charlie hoped it was sweet and peaceful, because the situation they were in was the opposite of that.

Lisa wanted to scream at it, wanted to pummel it into oblivion, but if she said something then it would take that as a sign of accomplishment and continue, like a bully that teased their victim repeatedly. It wasn't going to stop until they left or fought it. Before it could murder them like the rest who worked in the lab, who were trapped and lost; the others who were there to visit, steal, laugh at the torment the trapped went through. Horrible, cruel people who only wanted money for their own greedy desires, some people were like that in this world. The only thing she could do was not become one of those people and make sure the others didn't as well.

She heard quiet sniffling behind her, causing her to instantly look back, only to see Mitchell hiding his crying while he sat next to Sally; his friend who slept quietly. She hoped one of these situations wouldn't happen to her friends, but it was guaranteed.

"Hey, buddy, you alright?" Lisa asked in a mutter, wandering over to where Mitchell sat.

He looked up at her through his arms that were crossed over his knees, his blue eyes staring up at Lisa as the tears that craved freedom crossed past his freckles. He didn't answer, only placing his head back between his arms.

"Sally will be alright, you heard Millie. She just needs to rest," Lisa comforted, placing her hand on Mitchell's arm.

Mitchell lifted his head, slowly moving his eyes towards Sally, who still slept quietly.

"But she's been sleeping for so long, people don't take naps that much," Mitchell sniffled, the words struggling to leave his mouth.

Lisa couldn't think of anything else to comfort Mitchell. She hadn't been good at it ever and would usually just hope they wanted to be left alone. She sighed, sitting down next to Mitchell on the couch.

"Sally will wake up." The only words she could say escaped her finally.

He didn't buy that for a second. He wished he could, but too much had happened, and it affected him deeply. Lisa budged from her spot, leaving him to go back to the door. She continued standing there, a disappointing face taking over her, not because of him, but herself.


The room was quiet, even the wind's mist wasn't loud enough to be heard by human life. The bed was like the rest; a large purple blanket hung over the sides with a cold white pillow that always helped with sleeping. They couldn't even give these to the children they imprisoned, how sad.

Charlie sat quietly on the bed, stuffing her feet within the warm blanket. She looked up at the roof, contemplating what the sky looked like. She remembered that it was blue. She remembered all of it; she just wanted to see that again, but this project didn't allow them to have even a drop of outside. They isolated them and forced them to go through harsh conditions for their own needs. Cruel and horrible adults, who never cared about any of them. All the kids wanted was to see the outside world again, where the trees grew into beautiful giants. Where the clouds roamed above, watching as mankind went on with their lives. Where the rivers traveled throughout the world, one day reaching an ocean which took them to the waters. Where everything was free, where everything was peaceful, but it wasn't always like that, was it? They locked them away, shutting out any source of light the kids yearned for, begged for just one piece, and they couldn't even give them that. All they cared about was money, and that would be the thing rotting their lives forever. That thought made Charlie want to cry, how was money more important than innocent children? Who did nothing but want to just live their lives freely, who just wanted to run in a field and feel the wind kiss them on top of the face. Who just wanted a mother to hold them close, comfort them from their crying, help them through their lives to fulfill their dreams. None of that would have ever happened in the facility, where all they got was pain and screams that came along with it. It melted them away into a pool of nothing but depression and silence.

Charlie slapped her head, an attempt to get rid of those memories. Those memories that did nothing but destroy her into her own trauma that they constantly reminded her of. She let out a loose breath, laying down into a ball that she hoped would help her with her overloading thoughts.

The door to her bedroom opened, revealing Millie holding the door handle on the other side.

"Are you alright?" Millie asked, already knowing the answer.

"Yeah," Charlie responded, sitting back up as her green eyes met Millie's dark blue eyes, dark as the deepest layers of the sea.

Millie tramped over to the bed, taking a spot to sit down on the comfortable blanket. She tapped her feet against the floor, staring at Charlie, sooner or later the kid would give up. Then finally, she did.

"Okay, fine. I'm just…" She didn't want to say it. "…remembering what happened here." Her teeth grinded together in defeat, and the pain of those memories.

"I still hear them, everyone." Charlie squeezed her skin. "The screams...the pain and agony. They ruined me..." she choked out, coughing over her tears.

"They're gone, Charlie. They aren't able to hurt you anymore." She rested her hand on her shoulder.

"But it still feels like they can..." Charlie turned away, rubbing the tears from her face. The screams came back louder than ever. Sweat wept down her neck, her skin. The thing they cut into *over and over again.* She heard their cries, and within them, her own. Her friends, *everyone.* Her breath was louder and louder. It all came rushing back to her, to torment her, haunt her. Slicing, squelching flesh, her blood. Scalpels, needles, constant exhaustion, and tests.

'Experiment,' the word was like a snake bite on her tongue. That's all she was to them; they turned her into a rotting body, and there was no way back.

"Hey...Charlie. Look at me." She felt something squeezing her hand, as a voice pushed through all the noise.

"They're not real, not anymore." She remembered that voice. "Don't listen to it."

Charlie looked over at her friend sitting beside her; she now held both of her hands.

"They're loud, I know. They are haunting. And they will never go away, but...you're still here. You have fought against them for so long that you know they're not real. Those scientists, the people who hurt us...they aren't here anymore. We are. They never ruined us, we ruined them." Her breathing began to cool, and she felt her heart rate returning to normal. They weren't here anymore; her thoughts were just thoughts. They tried to hurt her. Her own mind was against her, but she shouldn't let it; it was her mind, after all.

"Breathe, I won't let it stop you or the others from freedom. Alright?"

Charlie was silent for a moment, before embracing her friend. "Thank you."

"Of course." Millie pulled away. "You remember what I said that one time?" Millie rested her head in one hand.

"You have to be more specific than that." Charlie shoved down a laugh. "You've said a lot of things."

"From the bible." Millie rolled her eyes sarcastically with a smile.

"Still more specific," Charlie whistled her words, smiling when she got a laugh out of Millie.

"The day Michael almost got electrocuted trying to get the door open."

"Oh..." Charlie's voice trailed off. "Yeah. I remember that day…what–did you say?"

*"You have angels protecting you. They won't let you die, and neither will I."* The specific memory wasn't easy to find, but the words were easy to remember. Charlie didn't know what to say, half the time she never understood, but this one was easy. They were inspirational from a path she couldn't find, something to live from. She remembered it wasn't directly about Michael almost electrocuting himself; Millie would obviously not yell at him like that for being very close to getting hurt.

"Oh, yeah," Charlie mumbled, the only word she was able to release.

Millie let her hand fall like a feather. She pulled herself up from the bed, heading back to the closed door.

"Please keep that in mind, alright, Charlie?" Millie begged calmly as she twisted the doorknob before stepping out of the room. Charlie nodded her head when Millie turned back. A smile went across her face as she exited, shutting the door behind her, because Charlie always wanted privacy. So, Millie would respect that.

Charlie stayed in the room for a while, checking on Sally occasionally. The kid was still asleep; the monster continued to slam its fists into the door. It was a determined thing; she wished that wasn't the case. It felt like they had been in the safe room for a while. There were no clocks anywhere, no way to see what time it was, or how long it had been. That's how it had always been. They never gave them access to it, to see when their suffering would end, or if it would ever would. She shook her head, her hair gliding on her face. She ignored it, her green eyes staring at them until she removed a strand from her vision.

She groaned, losing control of her head as it went face first into her curled up body. An annoying feeling angered her within. It was due to only herself, and she didn't know why, or where it even came from. It took over the thoughts of Millie's advice; it changed her thoughts of relief to sadness. Her friend's words were comforting, helpful for horrible occasions, yet it still hurt in those moments.

Sally opened her eyes to a bright, fuzzy light above her head, causing her to turn her head away and blink rapidly. Her forehead pounded, like a drum in a festival. She could hear the bang of the stick in her skin, like it was using her head as an instrument. Sally stuffed her face into the pillow she was laying on, pulling herself under the covers.

She heard footsteps coming closer to where she was laying; she didn't know who it was, but she didn't care.

"Sally? Are you awake?"

It was Lisa, coming to check up on her and see if she was up. Sally slowly unwrapped the covers, enough to where one eye was visible. She grumbled something in an annoyed tone, pulling the covers back over her head.

"She's up!" Lisa shouted across the room, celebrating it like some sort of holiday.

Sally heard running footsteps, then the sheet was yanked off her head; it was Mitchell.

"Are you okay?" he asked, his voice loud in her ears.

Sally was barely able to move her head, but she was able to strengthen herself enough to nod her head. Mitchell let out a long sigh of relief, loud enough to where Lisa thought it was herself.

"I will go get Millie," Lisa said, going into a trot as she ran around the corner to the bedrooms, where she had last seen Millie.

The banging jump scared Mitchell for some reason. He had gotten used to it before. He darted his eyes over his shoulder to the door that shook with every hit. Mitchell grumbled quietly, sitting down on the couch Sally was lounging on. The noise wasn't any better for her; it hurt her head as if it was slammed into a wall. She tried her best to block it from her ears, but it was pointless.

"She will be fine; it wore off," Millie said, releasing her hand from Sally's forehead.

"What about the headache she said she was having?" Lisa questioned.

"It's a side effect. It will go away in a little bit," Millie answered, facing her attention towards the kitchen. "Is anyone hungry?" she asked as she placed a hand on the countertop once she made it there.

Lisa chucked her chin up to Michael, gesturing him to go and ask Charlie. Michael saw through his sister's silent language and ran in the hallway, disappearing out of everyone else's sight.

The door to Charlie's room opened with Michael peeking in, almost tripping over something below him. It caught Charlie's attention, who giggled slightly.

The boy smiled awkwardly with embarrassment, trying his best to get rid of the smile so he could ask the question, "Are you hungry? Millie's looking for something for everyone to eat." Michael was able to put on a straight face.

"No," Charlie replied fast, catching him off guard.

"Oh, come on. You can't not be hungry after all of that," Michael retorted, opening the door fully.

Charlie didn't have any other response, so she threw herself from the bed. She sighed and followed Michael down the hall.

Everyone snacked on something small. It had felt like they weren't that hungry, but the group of children didn't realize how starving their stomachs were. A low rumble roared inside each one of them, small enough to where they couldn't hear it at all. Sally rested her head on the back cushions of the couch silently, munching on a banana. Mitchell sat next to her, chewing on the same fruit. The banging went on and on, each hit shaking something deep inside each one of them. All of them still feared it at that point, but they were so used to it; caring wasn't an option anymore. Besides Sally, who went into one of the bedrooms for a while after the bangs and screams had become too much for her.

Millie leaned on the countertops in the kitchen, finishing off the apple she had found. Sweet, not something the group had been given when the lab was still operating. The kids were glad that torture was over, but Millie knew that came with a cost, the rest of the children. Millie tossed the now yellow apple into the open trash can, almost knocking the garbage over. It caused Charlie to look behind her back; after not seeing anything suspicious, she turned back around and took a hard bite of the apple.

The room had brutal heat. Millie had tried to look for some sort of heater she could shut off, but there wasn't one in sight. She had given up a little while later after searching for what seemed like hours. Time had slowed down as they sat for ages in the safe room; even slower than the years they had spent together in the first. Charlie curled up on the couch, staring at her wiggling toes that couldn't stop moving on their own. Millie sat on the other end of the sofa, supporting Sally's words in her endless conversations while she fixed up her hair. It felt odd to see Sally with her hair down, since she had mostly worn pigtails the whole time she had been awake.

"Can we play truth or dare?" Sally suggested; everyone turned to her.

Lisa was the first to answer, "Yeah, sure. Once you are done."

The words made her grow less patient than she had been before. The kids hadn't played a game in a while, now might be the time when they still had the chance. An urge to do something to get their minds from the tragedy they were caged in, just something to do, to avoid the tormenting images of the beast outside.

"Can you do buns instead?" Sally asked, changing her mind from the original decision. "My mommy used to put my hair in buns all the time."

The words from the same child struck Charlie like the force of lightning. Her mother. That word forced itself into her head at the mention of it.

*Mother. Mother. Mother.* Millie noticed Charlie's expression, wide eyes with her arm covering her mouth.

"Are you okay, Charlie?" Millie's face went blank from its happiness a couple seconds ago.

Charlie whipped her head towards her. Dark, terrified eyes staring at her as if she was some sort of monster, like the one waiting to ambush them.

"Charlie?"

The girl blinked, confused, dilating her eyes. Reality hit her just then. It felt weird, like she was just gaining consciousness.

Sally looked at Charlie with concerned eyes. "Are you okay? Why are you staring like that?"

"I'm okay, sorry. I didn't mean to stare," Charlie mumbled with an awkward chuckle.

Considering the situation, it was like a miracle reaching the two. Millie continued brushing Sally's hair, starting to prepare it for the hairstyle the girl had suggested. Did Charlie still think it was her fault?


Millie squatted down in an empty space in the circle, joining the game when it was Charlie's turn to go.

Charlie let her thoughts pull her across the group of children, each one of them patiently waiting for a word to escape her mouth. A thought flickered in her mind like a lightbulb; it drew her over to Michael's eyes.

"Michael." She grinned, seeing the worried face Michael offered back.

"Truth or dare?" The expression on Michael's face was priceless; it was a piece of joy they could all have at this moment. Before Michael could answer, a realization occurred; the banging had stopped and had been quiet for a while now. It caught every slice of their attention; they all darted their eyes to the door.

"It could be tricking us. Maybe, we should wait it out for a little bit, just to be cautious," Millie warned, her voice suddenly serious and stern. It took a while for the group to release their eyes from the door, but eventually, they resumed their game.

"Dare." Michael smiled, yet that smile curved nervously.

"I dare you…" Charlie ended her sentence halfway through. She couldn't think of anything; no idea seemed to click through her brainstorming. Nothing was coming to her. She scratched a sudden itch between her hair follicles, like that would help her thinking. Then finally, something decided to show up.

"I dare you to dump some water on your head," Charlie dared.

Simple, yet fun. A comedic smile went across her face afterwards. Michael felt some sort of relief, and an emotion he couldn't pick out.

"Well, thank you Charlie. I actually do need that right now," Michael thanked the girl comically, standing on his feet as he went to the kitchen. He searched through the small fridge, immediately finding stacks of bottles of water. He plucked one out, stepping out of the kitchen so everyone could have a clear view of him. He struggled a little to pull the lid off. It fell to the floor after a short while. Michael didn't have a care in the world about picking it up. He raised the bottle over his head and poured. The water splattered everywhere, dripping down his dark hair and trailing down his white gown. Laughter came from the group. It made him smile as well. It felt relaxing and fresh; the safe room had been so hot. It was a moment of peace, for him, and for all of them. The water splashed against the floor, staining the carpets and letting it trickle down like a slope. It flew like an explosion as Michael finished off the water, his hair covering his eyes.

"Anyways. It's my turn," Michael said as he became part of the circle once again.

The water dripped everywhere, getting the people closest to him soaking wet. Millie suddenly handed him a towel, poking him with it until he took it. He thought of only where in the world did she pull it from? The only answer filling in the empty answer was thin air.

"Dry off first, you're literally drenching all of us," Millie stated, smiling back at the grin on Michael's face.

He plucked his head into the towel and began drying off.

"Where did you even get that towel from?" Lisa pondered everyone's thoughts out loud; they all looked over at her, comical suspicion tugging at their faces.

Millie let a smirk submerge from her face, a little chuckle following afterwards.

"Well, knowing how hot it is in here. Someone was going to dump water on themselves at some point," Millie explained.

She looked over at the now quiet door, examining and listening. She didn't buy the beast's tricks at all. Her glare at the door seemed to catch everyone's attention; they joined in less than a second.

"It's still there," Millie claimed, standing up on her feet. "We have to find a way around it."

"Don't you dare say it," Charlie said, no humor on her face and knowing every step of the plan Millie was thinking of already.

Millie focused her eyes on the door. Something was being planned in her eyes; they could all tell and knew what it was going to be.

"But you're already injured!" Charlie blurted.

"Let's try something different," Millie said, which was a shock to hear. Not a distraction; Charlie sighed with relief.

Millie sprinted off to the back of the hall. Lisa got up and stared down it, seeing the storage room wide open.

Millie got out with a red box in her hand, a toolbox. If she was right, then they could sneak around.

Millie wandered back to the door and crouched down, finding a hammer at the top of the pile of tools. The walls were unbreakable; she heard the floor in their safe room was the same material as the walls, so no one could escape. That was a new safe room recently built with that feature, but this one was much older.

Millie raised the hammer and loudly hit the floor, and she was relieved to see a dent where she marked it.

She struck repeatedly, like placing a nail in the floor. The group watched patiently, though some wanted to help badly, but that would be too much noise. The monster didn't need to know, or did it?

Millie hit again, as loud as she could, louder than their screams, their agony. She got up and put both hands on it, slamming it into the floor like she would with a sword.

No one even realized she was panting until she placed the hammer down gently, so as not to make any more noise. She went over to the door and put her ears against it, hearing no heavy breathing from it. It was gone; it had left.

Millie opened the door softly, and peaked her head out, staring in all directions to see if the coast was clear. When she confirmed there was nothing, the group snuck past whatever was there and bolted.

Their hearts pounded with each step, each breath; they stood close together past each room. The kids jumped at every sound. The monster was still here; it was searching wherever it thought they went after supposedly "hearing a hole being dug."

How long had it been since they left? Minutes, hours, there was no clock to tell them.

Millie spotted a door in the distance, one that looked familiar. She remembered using it once, to get to another section of the floor.

"Is the generator that way?" she whispered to Charlie, in case she was checking, which she probably was.

Charlie nodded her head; there were other ways, but this one was the closest.

The door was yanked open; she looked through every single detail, taking in everything in her sight. Millie stepped into the hallway, preparing a claw to slash across her face, or a monster to lunge on her, but she didn't see anything. It was nowhere in sight.

That's when she heard the heavy breathing above her. She slowly lifted her head, only to see the claws thrashing for her face. Millie hit the deck, making the monster fly into the door, breaking it off its hinges. Shock hit Charlie, how did she not see it?

Millie chipped a sharp stone from the crumbling wall as she was grabbed by the hair. The monster was in the way of their path to escape, their escape to freedom, that word, that word that they all wanted so much, so bad. But they wanted their friend back more than anything, and Charlie and Millie had a promise. Lisa yanked a rock off the ground, just as Charlie ran back towards the fight, watching as Millie got pummeled into oblivion with claws.

"Millie!" Charlie screamed, her voice registering in the monster's barely visible ears.

It bared its teeth as it snarled at Charlie, spreading its claws out in preparation of tearing a child apart. A rock rammed into the side of its head, and it tossed Millie to the ground.

The monster bolted at her; Millie ran after it with every ounce of courage she had inside of her once she got back to her scarred feet.

Charlie spotted a chair with a leg broken off lying right next to her. On instinct, she ripped it from its position and swung it, right as the monster reached her. The chair splattered with wood as it hit the target of the beast's head. It screamed, launching back into the ground again. Charlie wanted to run, wanted to take this as a chance to flee and help Millie out of here. Yet, something inside of her stopped her. Rage, for all the damage it had done. To her friends, to herself, to all the innocent lives.

She snatched the broken leg of the chair and lunged at the creature, landing right on top of it as she jammed the leg straight into its mouth, blood launching into her face. But she didn't care.

She didn't mind it at all. More slapped her in the face, drowning her in moist wet blood.

Charlie hadn't realized that Millie had hoisted her off the monster's body, dragging her away from it to save her.

Millie and Charlie ran as far as they could go. Charlie didn't realize Millie had already told everyone else to run. She used her powers, the walls beckoning to her eyes and seeing Lisa standing by a safe room door, waving her arms around in hopes Charlie will see her. The monster roared in its unbearable frustration, going after the kids in a heartbeat that it possibly skipped. The creature thrusted itself into the air and jumped on the wall, crunching the stone like it was sand on a beach, crawling as fast as a spider, ready to trap and eat its prey alive. Its white eyes were fixated on the girl's bodies. The amount of joy it would feel when these two were dead, scattered in bits across the ground, and the rest would be just as tormented.

Charlie had an idea clicking in her mind; the idea slowly flickering in her brain. She looked over at Millie, who was already staring at her. She nodded her head in acceptance that took so long to take when she saw the thoughts flickering in her friend's eyes. Acceptance of something dangerous she knew Charlie was carefully thinking of.

Charlie jumped through a wall beside her suddenly when the monster was focused on Millie. It was always focused on Millie since she had been fighting it all this time. It leaped off the wall, rocks tumbling around it like it was controlling them. Catching up to Millie, who slowed her pace on purpose before it lunged, extending its claw until it could reach the girl's head.

It couldn't; it didn't get the chance to.

Charlie leaped out of the wall, swinging a wrench that she held tightly in her hand and smacking the monster directly on the head with a clang, so hard that blood squirmed to be free from the hit. It's cold slim body fell to the floor, stopping like it was lifeless. It seemed so powerful, but so sensitive at the same time.

"How did you know what my plan was?" Charlie asked.

"I didn't really know...we should go!" Millie started to run faster down the hallway; Charlie followed closely behind.

The hallway was silent; their footsteps echoing right below them. The floor was just as messy as a garbage dump; every meter filled with some kind of rubble. Charlie constantly watched their backs, checking for their own safety in case it woke up and started to follow them like a predator. Hiding behind every corner to surprise its prey, but there was nothing, only the wisp of the wind behind her; neither of them knew where it was coming from.

"I wish there were some windows," Charlie mumbled to herself.

"Yeah, light would be needed in this place, but no one's going to use it once we get out of here. Unless someone buys it and renovates it for their own needs," Millie explained.

*Once.*

Millie used that word so passionately, like she was aware of the future and that they would escape, or it could just be her beliefs.

Charlie twisted a loose strand of hair in front of her. It was something to satisfy her after all they had been through; everything had happened so fast. The monster had appeared only ten minutes after they had escaped from the safe room, and it all went downhill from there. A deep breath was sucked in by Charlie; butterflies filled her stomach like water, water that boiled and hurt so badly. It hurt, hurt as much as everything in her life.

Millie looked empty, empty inside and out; her muscles controlled her like a machine, but she wasn't like that; she would never be. Her legs ached, about to cramp and give up on her. She pushed them desperately against their protests, cooling her breathing to encourage her own body to move forward.

Charlie turned to the hall behind them one last time before they reached the safe room. Lisa opened the door, waving and gesturing for them to hurry inside. Millie let Charlie go inside before she did. The oldest slowly closed the door behind her; everyone stared at her patiently, waiting for what to do next. Their heads were filled with nothing but fear; fear had found them and hadn't let them go in such a long time. It wouldn't until they left, all of them, once and for all.

Everyone slowly settled down in the nearest corner, comforting their bodies to rest for a little, before they left and ran for their lives again. Lives they all needed, but shocking that they still had them. Life had been so miscrable in the lab, so cruel, and the people who ruled lands that spread for miles were the ones who ran it all. The ones who wanted power, to kill millions of innocent lives, not just the ones in the wars, but the ones who were fighting for the sake of it.

That thought made Charlie gulp vomit down from her throat; it made her sick to her stomach, absolute sickness. She felt the waste clog her neck, but she shoved it back to her stomach, willing to bear the pain inside of her chest. Millie stood there silently in front of the group; it was a second, but it felt like infinity.

"Hey, Charlie?" Michael called out to her from across the room; he laid on the couch stomach-down.

"Hm?" she hummed to show she had his attention.

"That was awesome."

"Thanks."

It was silence after that; everyone recuperated themselves for the next endless battles ahead.

"If the generator is truly broken, then the stairs are the next option," Millie sternly said.

It was a terrifying plan; the stairs were a complete mess with the amount of people that ran down them for their lives. The monster probably followed them closely behind and finished off every human in its path. It was traumatizing itself to even think about, but the thought didn't leave Charlie's side, even if she wanted it to.

"Be careful once we're on the stairs. Anything could go wrong at any moment when we're out there," Millie warned before they left the safe room.

So, the group continued, awaiting whatever challenge the world decided to give them next.

# Chapter Twelve

Guilt Crushes the Minds of the Innocent

The stairs were long and steep, thousands of holes scattered across the layers and layers of them. Millie peered down, not daring to trust the handrail in front of her. Lisa looked over Millie's shoulders, groaning at the large number of floors they still had to go. She couldn't even see the bottom. Millie glanced at Lisa, she didn't give a glance back.

"I feel like we should take a different route, don't you think?" Lisa suggested, a nervous shake drowned her words.

"I wish we could take a different approach, but this is the only safe way. I'm not saying it's one hundred percent safe, but it's going to be safer than any other route we try to take, if there are other routes," Millie explained, crossing her arms as she heard the footsteps of one of the others walking up.

"Alright then," Lisa agreed finally. "But how are we going to navigate through this?"

She pointed a sarcastic finger down the stairwell, keeping her feet straight to balance. Michael stood by Millie's side now, crossing his arms to copy Millie's movements. Michael had no idea why he did it, maybe some way to be funny, to comfort her. Or maybe he wanted to feel important, like he had been doing something. He did, though; he was the only reason they had been traversing and making it.

What was he thinking? Why was he doubting himself?

"Are you okay, Michael?" Millie spotted his frantic eyes staring at all the imaginative questions inside his head.

"Yeah. I am fine," he laughed.

"Are you sure?"

"Yeah."

Millie turned back to what she was originally doing, but not before wondering what he was thinking about.

He let his arms fall to his sides, placing them on his hips as he stared at the entrance to the stairs they were about to cross. Lisa waved her hand at the other children, gesturing to them to come over.

The younger kids followed along. Sally made sure to stay in the middle of the group. It was always the safe spot, and she didn't want to go through that excruciating pain; she shivered at the slightest mention of it in her head. Millie stayed in front of the group, lowering her head to the first flight of stairs they would have to go through. The kids at her back waited to start the journey. Millie took the first step, and then the next. It seemed alright. The kids would be able to walk down safely: good.

Charlie stood in the middle, ending up right next to the youngest, Sally. It was insane how young some of the kids were in the facility, and how young the ones who died were. It was heartbreaking. It showed how far people would go for the sake of more money. Sally was only six-years-old. People were just cruel sometimes, and Charlie hoped that none of them would encounter people who were cruel and selfish if they escaped and saw the real world for the first time, from this giant prison. A prison of no peace, a prison of pain, a prison of isolation, depression, fear, everything she felt in those operating years was like the deepest pits of the dark; the darkness that surrounded her every second, the sounds of screaming following afterwards.

She hadn't realized she was zoning out and losing focus of her reality before she stepped through a loose stone. The floor below her foot crumbled, breaking into a hole big enough to fit a child like her. Charlie gripped the side of the stone, her hand scraping pain into itself as she held on tight. No one came to help, none of them. She tried to scream, but nothing escaped her mouth.

A shadow cast over the hole. A tall, familiar figure.

Charlie felt like crying, but the stern look of the shadow on her mother's face was cold and pale, *angry*. Nothing like the gentle and loving face she remembered. Her hands were clenched into fists, fists of built-up rage she had against someone; Charlie knew exactly who that person was. Her mother's foot crushed her hand underneath, blood pouring out of her broken skin. She was forced to let go, falling into the deep pit of pitch black below. Her body faded into the darkness, the light of the hole slowly disappearing into the black blanket that wasn't there before in the stairwell.

Charlie's hand was the only thing she could see, could feel, besides the tears pouring down her face. The blood on her hand was painful, but not as painful as seeing her mother crush her hand. She deserved it, anyway, so why was she scared? Why was she in pain? She should feel guilty of staying quiet, yet the pain overflowed in her body, her head, her eyes...

"Help!" she screamed, her voice only echoed into the dark. All she could see was darkness; the stairs hadn't been covered in a blanket of pitch black, right? Her breathing was heavy coming from her mouth. Not again, not again. She could see herself clawing in front of her, clawing at a door that was no longer there. She wasn't trapped anymore; she could escape this.

"Help!" the scream echoed again, nothing, no response to her sobs, her cries. "Please..."

Her mind snapped back to reality as her eyes opened, seeing her legs dangling into the stairwell that went on for ages. She lifted her head to the light above, seeing the hand of Millie holding on for her sorrowful dear life, whispering prayer after prayer for the sake of her soul. Everyone else was hanging on to Millie, forming in a line to save their friend. The poor girl lifted her other helpless hand, which Millie immediately latched onto, being able to pull her up and out of the hole.

Charlie sat up onto the safe part of the stairs, her body unable to move after all of that. What was that supposed to mean? Did her mother hate her in the afterlife? Or did she still love her like any caring mother would? Charlie thought about it every day, but it was a clear guess that she was no longer seen as the daughter of Ellie Utinew.

Charlie coughed something up that itched at her throat, her breath speeding in and out.

"Are you okay?" Millie asked; the dull light in her eyes was obvious.

"Yeah..." Charlie assured, taking one last deep breath. "I'm okay." Did her mother hate her? The question stirred again and again, and it wouldn't go away.

The children moved on from the incident, escaping the thoughts of it while they walked slowly down the stairs; they were sure to now be careful of any loose pieces of the stone.

Millie turned the corner to the next stairs, her mind becoming frustrated and furious. Her jaw clenched as she turned back to the path they were taking.

The flights of stairs, or what used to be stairs, were filled with a giant hole, separating them from the next level; they would have to go to the floor they were on.

"We can't go any further," Millie revealed as soon as the kids saw the hole. The sign to their only option stood firmly by the door.

*Floor twenty-five.*

Lisa grasped the knob of the door to the next floor, opening it carelessly. She realized it and anxiously shaped and twisted a picture of the monster roaming the floor already. The door slid open fully, screaming like a banshee in the cold night. The level was like the rest, destroyed into nothing but the crumbs of the past massacre. The only living thing remaining was the rats that ran across the halls.

Lisa stepped through the doorway, entering the silent floor that was covered in the smell of dried-up blood and dust. Old, ruined, it had been destroyed. Millie went through next, exploring the area with only her eyes.

"Do you think the generator works?" Lisa wondered; her thoughts became words, which ran over to Millie.

"Maybe, I'm not sure," Millie said, wiping some dried-up blood off her shoulder with her fingers.

Charlie appeared by Millie's side, having no plans to speak a single word. Exhaustion was tackling her. After all the times she had used her power, it had drained her from any energy she used to wield.

Her head thumped with a pounding spell, banging at her brain that felt like it was mentally broken. Charlie placed a hand on her forehead, as if that would help with the miserable headache that she couldn't deal with for that much longer. Charlie saw Millie examining the ceiling; the stone was filled with spiderwebs of cracks. It could fall on them any minute.

"It would be best if we started searching or at least find a roof that doesn't look like it's about to crumble to pieces." Millie pointed to the stone over their heads.

Lisa nodded her head in agreement, looking over at Charlie, who only nodded at least an inch. The headache was too much, but she would have to deal with it for now.

Mitchell peeked through the doorway, checking to see if it was safe or not. He didn't know why he did that. If Millie and the other two were just standing there, then obviously it was safe. He slowly crept through the door, startling Charlie for a second before she went back to focusing on the pain in her head. Her neck started to hurt as well, always having to twist or turn. It felt like her own neck that supported her throughout everything was strangling her. Charlie grumbled, holding another hand on her neck.

"Are you okay, Charlie?" Lisa was the first to notice.

"Yeah, just a headache," Charlie answered.

Mitchell stood behind Lisa, looking past her arm and at the hall in front of them.

Her head wanted to be let out so badly; she wanted to scream, but she held them back, because screaming now might be her last, and she would rather live.

It was quiet, too quiet. Silence had caught up with them, hugging them tightly and not letting them go. Millie whispered to the others to come over, silently. If a silent atmosphere was preferred more to survive, then they might as well add to it. Being a noisy voice wouldn't be appreciated besides the beast locating them. The kids huddled in a circle; none of them even considered turning their backs on an open area. A quiet layer of whispers crept throughout each inch of the walls surrounding them, coming closer like the waves of a tsunami.

Charlie had that feeling again; her stomach felt like it was about to burst into blood, but it wouldn't, because that wasn't possible right now. She knew Millie felt the same; her eyes were darting around the room swiftly, swift as an eagle looking for its dinner. She was sort of like an eagle when Charlie thought about it, fighting for their freedom, protecting them, and shielding them from anything harmful.

A crack appeared on the ceiling, shaping and forming itself into a spiderweb. As if an invisible spider was doing the work to catch some sort of prey, was it a display to distract them? Keeping their attention for the true predator to attack? Charlie couldn't tell, and Millie doubted the monster would jump through it when everyone had their eyes locked onto the ceiling of the oncoming hole. It continued, spreading across the ceiling rapidly, mist falling from the roof, blobs of fog flowing through the hallway. It stopped right over their heads, causing the kids to move instantly. It went silent again; the cracks ended, and the mist vanished into nothing.

"Is it—"

Mitchell had no time before the monster burst through the ceiling, catching the poor child in surprise. Millie didn't have a chance to save him when the monster swung, hitting him directly in the chest. Blood sprayed out of it like a broken pipe full of water. The kid fell to the floor, slamming into the cold, blood stained stone.

The monster stood over Mitchell, the shadow so menacing as it covered the poor kid's body. It raised a claw, the dried blood glistening in the lit-up room coming from nowhere. It was only able to swing air when Lisa shoved it away and out of reach from her friend.

She trailed after Millie, who carried Mitchell to safety with the rest. She was so fast, it didn't even notice her whisking him away.

# Chapter Thirteen
## The Anger of an Experiment

Mitchell was held tightly in Millie's arms as she sprinted along with the other kids. The monster was not that far behind them, lunging into nothing on each side of the hall. It somehow wasn't getting tired, like it was an experienced player of a game. The rest of the kids felt like they were about to tumble through the floor. Charlie looked back at the monster, so much hate and wrath was in her mind at that thing. The countless thoughts of murdering it went on forever, boiling inside of her, but she wouldn't be able to kill it; even if the rage deep inside of her pounded at her peaceful thoughts. It wasn't uncontrollable, and she wouldn't let it get the best of her, so no one else would be hurt because of her emotions.

Charlie felt her legs shaking with each step, her feet were starting to wear out on her; they were almost about to collapse. She couldn't go on any further, but she had to. She had to for the sake of her life, and the lives of the others. One leg almost stumbled on her, but she was so tired, she couldn't continue. Her other leg almost fell over; she had to keep her feet pushing, for herself and the group. The monster kept close behind but not close enough to swing. Charlie's legs were giving out; the energy in her body was draining. It had already been drained, how was she still running?

They couldn't run forever. If she was giving out, then some others might be as well; she had to stop it, to give them some time.

Out of some pure miracle, she spotted something deep within a mountain of rocks.

A gun buried in some rubble. She gripped it through a hole in the rocks, yanking it out and stopping dead in her tracks, not waiting to see if they stopped for her. Millie turned around after not noticing Charlie's figure in the group; her eyes widened with horror. She stopped herself from sprinting, since Mitchell still lay limp in her arms.

"It might not be loaded!" Millie warned.

Charlie didn't respond, her eyes too focused on the thing to answer her friend.

It galloped for the girl, forgetting to consider the dangerous weapon gripped in her hands. The trigger clicked just as it was about to maul her to death. She fired, the bullet flowing smoothly through the air at the speed of lighting before breaking its way through the skin of the monster's shining eye.

The blood started pouring out of its eye once again, the eye it had just regenerated, the eye it had used to slaughter thousands. Charlie didn't feel guilty for even a second; it had gotten what was coming. A scream pierced their ears, a siren that told them it would kill them, and it would do it over and over if it had the chance to.

Charlie ran back towards the group, realizing the gun had no bullets left, making it useless. She tossed it to her side, leaving it there to lay silently, to be covered up after nature took over.

Mitchell was still alive, the bleeding from the scar had stopped due to Millie's power, but Charlie could tell she was getting tired too; her knees buckled for a split moment.

The kids turned a corner, the monster leaving their sight, all of them wished it was permanent. Maybe it would, maybe they would leave this place, and lock this thing inside to rot for how long it would live. Charlie hoped it was painful; she hoped it would always be in pain, in constant agony that would beat it forever. This hate inside of her pulled her down, but she shoved through it. She pushed it away, focusing on what was important, the safety of her friends, and getting out of this hell.

It wasn't intentional to shoot the monster straight into the eye, but it worked and bought them some time. That's all that mattered.

Charlie noticed a twitch in Mitchell's eye; the lid slowly slid open, the blue eye revealing itself from its rest underneath.

"Can you stand?" Millie asked, being the second one to notice his awakening from his slumber, setting his feet down on the ground, but she didn't let him go yet in case he fell.

"Yeah," he mumbled. He was able to walk perfectly fine. Yet an uncomfortable taste lingered on his tongue, like getting burned by fresh food. He got burned by something far worse though.

The group ran, as fast as they could run, killing the exhaustion that had been torturing them forever, inside their heads, and in their legs. Walls of cracked stone watched their shadows flee across it, through the messy floors, through the darkness surrounding them. Charlie pointed out the directions to the generator, like she had been doing. The headache wasn't as bad as before, enough to give her space to do what she needed to do. Eventually, they stopped in front of the machine.

Michael opened the door, but it stopped halfway through. He pushed harder, shoving his entire body into it. Something groaned on the other side when he slammed again; it still didn't budge. Millie stepped in, bracing herself before slamming straight into the door, opening the metal so fast, like she had scared it into opening. A shelf had been stopping the door, like someone had put it there, unaware that the attacker could go through walls. There wasn't a body in the room, just the generator.

"Let's hope this one isn't completely…" his voice trailed off into thought. "What's the word again?" Michael stopped to think.

"Messed up?" Lisa suggested.

"Yeah, messed up. Something like that," Michael said awkwardly.

He slid into the floor and crawled on his knees. There was a hole at the side of it, again.

"Why are there always giant holes on the side of these? Literally all of them have one?" Michael asked, knowing very well not a single one of them had an answer or explanation.

"If it is a coincidence, I have no clue. But maybe it's not, maybe someone placed those there on purpose," Millie responded.

It seemed obvious in some way, the answer slipping from the tip of his tongue to never be thought of again. Michael stuck his head inside and started searching,

"Do we still have the flashlight? Or did we accidentally drop it during one of the attacks?" Michael's voice was muffled and far away in the generator.

"I dropped it, sorry," Millie apologized, sighing in disappointment.

"That's fine," Michael assured. "I can see just fine in here anyway."

That was a lie, he couldn't see a thing; everything was covered in the pitch-black blanket of the darkness, he would have to feel. He squeezed his hand through, touching everything that encountered his fingers.

"Are you sure you can see in there?" Millie noticed the obvious, chuckling softly.

"Yep, I got it."

Another lie, a pretty obvious one too.

"No, you can't Michael." Lisa rolled her eyes. "Just stop lying, there literally isn't a point."

"Yeah," Millie sighed under her breath with a smile. "Hold on." She walked over to the other side of the generator, crouching down onto her knees.

Millie found a loose piece of whatever the generator was made of. She found a small hole at the bottom, so she put her fingers through, lifting the piece of material from the generator.

"There, more light," Millie said as she met Michael's eyes when she plucked her head through.

"Was it that hard to ask for?" Lisa snickered.

"Okay, Lisa. The jokes over." Michael plucked his head out.

"Never heard you say that before." He rolled his eyes at her comment.

"I wouldn't be surprised if we found out you were the one punching holes through all of the generators." Michael changed the topic, finally being able to see clearly in the darkness that once evaded his vision.

"And why would I do that?" asked Millie.

"I don't know, maybe you were bored or something."

"That's a weird way to pass the time," Charlie laughed quietly. The group was silent as Michael worked afterwards.

Millie still sat at the other end of the generator, helping Michael out in his observation on the machine. Michael swung his hand around, almost smacking Millie directly in the face, but due to that, he also knocked something onto the floor. The machine started operating again, so Michael and Millie quickly lifted their heads out of the hole.

"Done," Michael congratulated himself silently, raising a quick thumbs up.

Charlie clapped her hands together quietly, a small smile growing across her face. It quickly vanished into a small line.

The group started to head back to the elevator, focusing on their surroundings, taking every detail of the spots around them. Their thoughts couldn't even be somewhere else. Their attention was stuck to the area like glue, each noise, each sound, everything was important, absolutely everything. Rocks scooted out of their way with a gentle kick. Millie walked at the front; zero emotion was mixing around in her eyes. Her expression was still, dull, like she was sad about something. Charlie already knew what, but it still hurt to see. Her dark blue eyes were moving slightly, flowing like the deep part of the ocean. Every radio of noise was worthy of being aware of.

A loud bang, just right ahead of the group, a low rumble of a growl following afterwards. The group knew what to do in this situation, knew what that monster was capable of, yet it was as if it were the first time all over again. None of them bolted back; they didn't pick up a weapon or something to defend themselves. Their bodies froze in terror, like fear was a whole new experience for them. Millie didn't have time to tell the kids to get out of sight or hide before the monster turned the corner. Its teeth grinded in excitement; excitement of a satisfaction long awaited ever since it met the kid, ever since it first saw them. All it could think about was its teeth sinking into their screaming skin. Millie sighed, more annoyed than terrified at this point; she had survived countless times with this thing, from the first and soon to be the last. She pressed a hand against her forehead.

"Get everyone somewhere safe, then find the elevator. I'll meet you there again," Millie whispered, knowing the last statement was going to be right, not out of confidence, but out of pure experience of battles and small wars.

"Millie, you promised..." Charlie reminded, making her way through the group to face her.

"It's not like that, not this time." Millie turned to the monster, not looking her in the eyes.

Lisa listened with a bit of hesitation, gently shoving Sally backwards, an attempt to silently tell her to go. Sally got the message immediately, running through the group; the rest of them followed right behind. Once she saw them run out of sight, once she didn't hear their voices trailing into her ears anymore, she spoke.

"You remember me, don't you?" Millie asked, her eyes more intimidating than the monsters. It nodded, making it obvious that it still understood the language it once spoke long ago. The monster rounded the corner, crouching on its two legs and hands.

"You're still angry with me, right?" Another question was spit out of her mouth. "You want me dead. All of us are brats to you."

It didn't nod that time; it only stared at her with hateful eyes.

"If you hurt another one of them. I swear, I will kill you, and you won't be able to use that power you so desperately wanted."

It bared its teeth, but no snarl or growl matched it.

"This is a warning, if one of them dies. I promise you..." Millie took a deep breath, her fists clenching as she stepped a bit closer to it. "Your ego won't be the only thing hurt when you took this job."

And just like that, she was gone.

The threat had no lie intended inside. That threat was a promise, and she wouldn't break it; she knew her words wouldn't go against anything ever. She knew her hands would be full of that thing's blood at some point; her fingers would be dripping of the red liquid that sustained a body, a body of a human, and a beast that had murdered with no mercy. She hated the thought of it, but negotiating was out of the question. As she stormed her feet to where the kids were, she planned to steady her steps, to calm herself, her fear.

One fear was her wheel for this life, the one thing that had kept her going for so long. Losing them, that had haunted her for the whole time she had spent with them. The first time she saw them, when she saw everybody in that facility, her fear was losing them, and she had lost so many of them thanks to that beast. Deep down, something told her it wasn't her fault, but Charlie's confirmation was the last thing she needed to fight against that thought deep inside her.

That monster, who chose this path himself, didn't regret it one bit. Even if she couldn't understand him, couldn't understand him at all. She knew deep down that he enjoyed every second of his slaughter, every minute of the murder that occurred while they hid away. It was for their safety, but it was such a big cost in the end.

She placed her hand on the curved wall, peering down the hallway ahead of her. Silence, pure quiet, even her breath was heard by nothing, not even herself.

She didn't hear the footsteps of the monster behind her; it seemed to not follow her. It didn't look scared when she spoke to it, so that couldn't be the reason. She probably wouldn't know ever, since she couldn't understand its growls and roars; all she could do was focus on body language, and it barely did that sometimes. Millie wasn't scared of it anymore...just tired, anxious for the kids' safety. She knew murdering it was the only way for it to finally leave them alone.

"Millie just looked annoyed, not really...scared, don't you think?" Michael asked Charlie as they silently crept through the hallway.

"Yeah, I think she's just tired of it at this point," Charlie said, looking back at the hallway they had just walked through. "We all are."

"Will she be okay?" Sally jumped into the conversation.

"I'm alright," a voice that wasn't following them before said, causing them all to stop in shock and surprise.

They all whipped around at once, only to see Millie strolling down the hallway unharmed. Not a single scratch in sight; not a flinch of pain was altering her movement. There hadn't been a fight at all.

"Are you okay?" Lisa ran to her, just wanting to reassure herself and everyone.

"I'm okay," Millie responded, her smile dull yet assuring.

"Are we continuing? Or do you all want to take a break?" Millie suggested two choices, the most cheerful and respectful child, like that serious mood had just vanished from her; it wasn't surprising. Millie was always like this. Yet, this time, it felt odd, like she was trying to delete the thoughts of that beast that might have followed her or not; she doubted it did though. A smile was spread across her face, that gentle, kind smile that they all loved and adored.

The group decided to move on; they were close to the elevator, according to Charlie, so might as well head over there then instead of risking getting attacked by the monster.

It was quiet amongst the group; it was normal, and no one had the urge to talk about something cheerful anyway.

The elevator was right ahead of them, waiting just at the end of the hall. This had been a challenging floor, pure fear and running. Millie pushed the button, still silent as ever. It lit up under the pressure, then they had to wait. The silence needed to be covered; the ominous whisper of the wind was too much for the children.

"I know now is a bad time to say this, but this is a good spot to get ambushed," Michael muttered, standing beside his sister. He knew he could've said something more comforting, and he regretted it instantly when it slipped from his mouth.

"Don't jinx it please," Lisa said, nudging him comedically afterwards with a smile, but he knew hidden under that smile was fear.

It didn't come, no jumpscare, no ambush, just pure silence as the doors opened, inviting the group inside. Millie waited for everyone else to go in first, eyeing the area around them in case it decided to attack. Still there was nothing, so she entered the elevator last, watching the hallway for the last time before the doors blocked her vision of the floor they would never see again.

# Chapter Fourteen

Trickery

"**H**as anyone been keeping track of how many floors we have gone through?" Lisa asked, standing in the closet corner to the elevator doors.

They all looked at each other, hoping for someone to speak out. Charlie activated her power, knowing that this was risky since she would be exhausted and would barely have the strength to run. But she did it anyway, raising her head towards the roof, and seeing the safe room they had started at. The rooms were completely overlapped with each other; she couldn't tell how many. Charlie sighed, noticing the group staring at her, waiting for an answer.

"I can't tell, sorry," Charlie apologized, sitting down on the cold hard floor, the weary ache of her legs pushing her down into whatever depths it wanted her in.

Millie stood up. "I think we have gone down fifteen floors, if I recall right..." She then seemed to realize something; Mitchell noticed the expression on her face.

"How long has this elevator been going for?" she asked everyone who heard it.

The others had only just registered it when Millie had said it. Some darted their eyes around, as if the answer was around them, but all they saw was the torn apart walls of the elevator. The numbers on the elevator had been damaged, unusable, and unreadable.

"I hope this goes down to the first floor," Michael uttered, sitting in front of the elevator.

They continued waiting, but the elevator didn't stop; it wasn't halting.

"Is it just going to go forever, until it reaches the first floor?" Mitchell asked, how much of a miracle that would be. It just kept going, going on and on. No one spoke after the recent conversation; they all waited and waited, waiting for the next chapter of this story that no one knew the ending of. Millie stood in front of the elevator, she stared at it like it was God Himself, admiration, respect.

"Are you alright, Millie?" Lisa asked; her voice drowned in concern and worry. Millie looked over her shoulder; her dark blue eye shaped in a stern and serious tone.

"I'm fine, just waiting," Millie mumbled, looking back at the elevator. Millie rested her arms in a cross across her chest, a comfortable position for however long they would be in the elevator.

Charlie took a quick glance at her; she stood there quietly, like she was a security guard on a night shift, quiet, maybe bored? Charlie probably would never know, would never understand what she was thinking, something wise probably.

The elevator came to a stop; the kids went dead silent, watching as the doors slid open, and the new floor emerged.

"This isn't the first floor, unfortunately," Millie called out, hating to ruin their excitement.

Millie stepped through but kept her foot on the floor of the elevator, in case the doors decided to close on them. It was unlikely, but this place was also unpredictable, and she didn't want to risk someone standing alone in a place full of horrors and a monster that took pleasure in erasing life. Mitchell went through first, then Sally. Charlie was next, then Michael, and finally, Lisa. The doors to the elevator closed right afterwards, as if they would operate anymore. Charlie froze when she faced the elevator one last time. Her reflection froze right in front of her. She stared at the fake mirror, watching her green eyes carefully, as if it would jump out at her, ambush her.

"Charlie?" Millie stepped beside her; she saw her reflection through the doors as well.

"I just haven't seen myself in a long time," Charlie claimed.

There hadn't been a mirror in the safe room, not even the bathroom. Charlie wiped a follicle of hair away from her eyes. She swiftly turned around and walked towards the group. Millie joined her, falling into step beside her as they put themselves in the puzzle of the small group of humans. It wouldn't be complete though, and only one was aware of that.

The group moved on from the elevator, already knowing the next part of the plan: look for the generator, get back, and find the new elevator.

"Have you all ever wondered why this place operates like this?" Michael wondered, saying his thoughts out loud.

"What do you mean?" Millie was the first to respond.

"Like, why do all the elevators operate off the generators on each floor? And why are there so many different elevators when there could've just been one?"

"Maybe, one elevator wasn't enough?" Lisa barged into the conversation.

"If there was a problem, they wanted a generator on each floor. So, they didn't have to go to a specific floor in order to fix the elevators," Millie explained, ending the conversation quickly.

The generator was hard to find; the place was crumbling into nothing but bits of the walls and floor. Rubble was scattered everywhere; each spot of the floor had to be filled with something. Eventually though, Charlie was able to see it through the walls, and they ventured over.

"These generators are also weird, not the ones I remember from our house," said Michael as he examined the inside, searching for the problem that they all seemed to have.

All the kids sat far away while Michael did his magic, as he squirmed and felt everything in his reach. Millie had punctured another hole in the generator to help him out a little. She was now leaning against the wall, watching him to make sure he didn't get hurt, even though he had done this plenty of times before. That incident back in the safe room was still stuck with her. It haunted her every night.

A click hit the ears of each one of them, causing them to turn to Michael who had his head plopped into the hole, he struggled to get out, but soon they saw his brown eyes again,

"Got it." A smile went across his face; he seemed to forget about the horrors that he had experienced over an unknown time limit, but that thought would take over again, and that smile would disappear. How long had they been running? How long had they been hiding? The kids would never know, not until they saw the sky outside. The daylight or the moonlight, whichever one they see, is the one they start their new life on.

"What do we do when we get out?" Charlie was the first to say something after a quiet walk back to the elevator.

Millie looked over her shoulder. "Maybe get adopted, go to school, wherever life takes you."

"But what if the government just puts us in another lab?"

That question had everyone stop dead in their tracks; it made Millie turn fully to the young girl. She didn't have anything to say, she wasn't going to lie, and it was obvious she couldn't think of some way to tell Charlie the horrid possible truth in good words.

Finally, an answer left her mouth, "I don't know what they're going to do, but if they try this again, I will fight off every last one of them if it means protecting you all," Millie promised. "And then I will burn this place all the way to hell."

The small part of the journey afterwards went silent again. Everyone was too busy thinking if Millie was going to defend them against armies. Even though she would always stand by her word, would she be able to do it? That question was big, and all their minds were filled with one hopeful word:

*Yes.*

The area around them was quiet, quiet as a field on earth, but it wasn't the good kind. Millie had that feeling in her chest, but she wasn't serious in her surroundings. It didn't feel like an attack, a bad feeling, but not an ambush. The silence was messing with her head, and she didn't enjoy it one bit.

Charlie had the same feeling; she was squirming to see what was haunting her, yet she couldn't see it. Anxiety forced her to see the thoughts of it, unlike Millie, who didn't look frightened about the sense. She was worried, and it was obvious to see. Her teeth were clenched with her jaw; she felt her whole body sweating with anxiety, worry, stress. It all squeezed her tight with all the strength it possessed.

Millie was the first to step around the corner, but once she turned her head, the first thing she did was step back, grabbing the closest to her and setting them down on the floor, Lisa was the target.

"Get down," Millie whispered, intensity filling her voice's vocal cords. Everyone plopped down on the cold stone floor.

"What?" Michael whispered as loud but also as quiet as he could, being one of the kids at the back of the line.

"The monster?" Lisa said back, wondering what other reason he could think of that would make Millie hit the deck. She peered around the corner again, eyeing the beast, who was just standing there, stiff as a rock on a mountain.

"What's it doing?" Lisa asked, slowly crawling behind Millie to peek around the corner as well, making her question useless words that had no real reason coming out of her mouth.

The monster looked down at its feet, but Millie quickly realized something on the floor was really intriguing to it. It took a step forward, and before Millie could comprehend the situation, the thing phased right through the floor.

"Oh," Millie muttered, standing to her feet as she entered the giant room the monster was once in. Those words hit like a hammer to the rest of the kids.

"What?" Michael asked in worry. "Millie, where did it go?"

"It just jumped through the floor," Millie said. It wasn't a surprise.

"Why would it..." His sister guessed it wasn't in a comedic manner as he spoke it.

Charlie thought about those words; a sudden realization hit her: she could do that too. She could've done that all along; she felt like slapping herself for that thought, she would never want to leave her friends behind, never. Besides, she would have nowhere to go anyway, and she would be completely defenseless. The thought was washed away in her head, so she could focus on the right thing at that moment. The ocean swerved smoothly in her mind, countless ideas forming like the colonization of a community. She hadn't noticed everyone leaving for the giant main room. Millie's face appeared from around the corner, seeing Charlie still squatting on the ground, her eyebrows raised with confusion.

"Are you coming?" She fully stepped into the hallway.

"Yeah." Charlie lifted herself to her feet.

"Daydreaming?" Millie guessed, a sweet smile on her face.

"I guess?" The girl raised her arms in a confused manner with an awkward smile spread across her lips. She trotted past Millie to join the rest of the group. She switched back to wondering about what the monster did? Why did it leave so soon? Did it know they were here? Then it struck her like a bolt of lightning. It was trying to trick them. When they exited the elevator to the next floor, it would be waiting to attack them, an ambush.

"It's trying to trick us," Millie said aloud, swinging everyone's attention directly to her.

"Huh?" Michael's eyebrows rose up.

"It's trying to surprise us. It's going to wait at the elevator when we enter the next floor and attack us, like it was guarding the safe room."

Millie sighed, stepping closer to her friends ahead of her, "We will have to find a different route."

"Are the stairs still available?" Lisa suggested the question, looking around to see if the stairs were anywhere near them; they were not. Millie didn't hesitate to give the same suggestion in response.

"Maybe, we could find them and see if they're busted or not." She waved her hands in the same motion her words exited. So, the group ventured off into a hopeful way to their freedom.

"Dang it." Lisa's eyes widened with disappointment.

The stairs were destroyed and unusable. Millie stood beside her, a loose breath of disappointment escaping her mouth.

"So, I'm guessing they're useless." Charlie walked up from behind, some of her sassiness taken from Michael.

"Yep," Millie said, an unhappy smile across her face.

"So, what do we do now?"

Millie's face suddenly turned surprised, as if they had just thrown her a surprise birthday party; she looked over at Charlie.

"Don't even say it," Charlie pleaded aggressively; her hands were clenched together into fists. "Please." Her teeth were grinding like gears, forcing themselves together to stop her bad idea.

Lisa knew the expression on Millie's face; she was about to fight it again, everyone around her could tell.

"If we can surprise it with a weapon of some sort from above, we could knock it out and run away," said Millie. She also had another idea, but they wouldn't accept that one, not yet.

"But what if it doesn't get knocked out?" Charlie asked.

"You knocked it out with a wrench, anything stronger than that could probably work." She proudly smiled, but it wasn't for herself, Charlie didn't have any other option but to smile back.

It took the group a long time to find where the monster was waiting underneath. Charlie got exhausted after a while, so the group stopped for breaks for the poor girl's sake, even though Charlie insisted that she could just activate the power and not stop. Millie told her to quit it after some point, because she was barely able to stand.

"There," Charlie stated, pointing to the floor as she crouched down, her legs buckling from a sore ache.

Millie crouched down next to her, examining the floor as if she could see through it.

"Michael, you have more strength in your legs than anywhere else, right?" Millie asked, turning to Michael suddenly.

"Huh? Well–I don't know—"

"What number is on your hand?" Michael was still confused at her sudden question, but he looked down at his palm.

"Fifty-Seven?" he said, waving his hand.

"Okay, do you know how to use it?"

Michael could barely comprehend words to say, even though he already knew his answer. "No? I didn't even know what mine was. But that would explain a lot...how do you know that anyways?"

"I knew all of the kid's powers in this place, before they…" She cut off the sentence there, sighing out of a sudden thought of pain, sadness. Everyone assumed Millie didn't want anyone to mention it.

"Try to tighten the muscles in your legs," Millie ordered, hoping he would follow it. "That should activate it."

Michael was willing to follow along with the plan; he was just shocked at the fact that Millie knew his power before he could even realize he had one. Of course he did; he just never discovered it until now apparently.

"So, what's the plan?" Michael spoke as he walked over to where Millie and Charlie were crouching.

"Can you try and break the floor?" Millie's face was focused with her dark blue eyes; he guessed she wanted his approval before they went along with it.

"I'll try."

Millie searched the room; her eyes found a sign.

"Weaponry," it read, she thanked God for that one.

She lifted herself to her feet and walked over, squeezing through the door and out of sight.

All the guns were either dead or not loaded with no ammunition in sight. So, it wasn't long before she came out with a metal bat clenched in the palm of her fingers.

The monster lurked, searching for the elevator it couldn't see. The floor was cluttered with rubble it had caused, yet it still felt no remorse despite its frustration. The thought of leaving had been on its mind for a while now. Yet it knew and was sure that the second it attempted havoc; it would be gunned down by thousands before it even stood a chance. This lab was the one place it had power above all.

It fell forward intentionally, landing on its hands in a swift motion. The beast started moving, scanning the area ahead to figure out where to go next. But then there was a sound, rumbling, a slam. It squirmed around from the scare, searching its surroundings in its jumps of anxiety. The slam hit again, only shaking the monster's frustration higher up its body. It couldn't find the source of this sound; it was frightening and frustrating at the same time. Again, the slam shook the room around it, causing it to almost fumble into the ground. The mouth with the milk white teeth covered in red screamed in its torment of anger. The wrath of the hit caused it to bare its teeth, still jumping around and turning in all sorts of directions.

Another bang, like the shake of an earthquake. It roared, scratching the ground with its claws. The shake of the scream was larger than the rumble it had been experiencing; silence fell, complete silence. It swirled around the beasts barely seen ears, allowing no noise to be heard.

The ceiling shattered like the glass shards of a window, Millie appearing from within it with a metal bat raised over her shoulder. Stones tumbled through her jump, hitting the monster constantly. It thrashed about, slashing Millie in the face, barely missing her eye. She didn't back down, swinging the bat into the monster's neck. Blood leaked from the holder of its head, swerving down to its stomach. Millie jammed it in even further as she landed on top of the monster's body while she held it down through the air. A dark red river splattered, racing to catch up with the rest of the stomach.

"Run! Now!" Millie yelled to the kids as they were able to land onto the floor safely; she jumped off the beast to join them, to run with the bat in her hands, in case it got up, but when she felt that tug on her hair. She realized it was needed.

The kids didn't seem to notice how she was being held by her own hair, while they ran away on Millie's orders. Michael being dragged by his sister Lisa. Millie felt the bat leave her grip, as it clattered to the floor.

"Millie!" she heard Charlie shout from the hall.

She glared up from where she was caught, seeing Charlie start bolting towards her, Lisa was running behind her.

"Don't! Go!" she screamed, trying to lodge the creature's hands off her head.

The monster jolted, throwing her through the air in a swift snap of its arms. Wind clawed at her face, like nails digging into her skin.

Millie hit the floor with a loud slam; she was able to get up quickly before the monster could lunge directly onto her, scrambling out of the way, and watching as the monster stabbed its claws into the ground. It caught Charlie running towards it, and the kid stopped in the hall within its vision. It roared and prepared to charge at her next, but its leg buckled as a bat hit its knee.

The beast whipped its head to Millie, its bright glowing eyes staring directly into her soul deep down inside of her. It hated the light she had, the faith, the strength that overpowered it in every way. It hated her with anger so big it forced it into blind rage it had started itself so long ago.

"I'll meet you two wherever you go, just run, please," she pleaded, watching Lisa and Charlie hesitate. "Please."

Millie blinked at Charlie and nodded her head. This wasn't a sacrifice; she had a plan, but it was solo. The two girls took a breath in and nodded their heads back, running off with the rest of the group who had that same mindset.

The beast snarled aggressively, baring its teeth that were stained with her own blood.

Millie wasn't affected by it, raising the bat over her head before swinging again, smacking it over the skull.

The monster screamed, breaking something inside of Millie's ears. A searing pain grasped onto every part of her skin inside of her head. She ignored it since she saw through the monster's distraction attempt. It jumped for her, but she was able to dodge it, staggering to the side as the monster slammed into the wall. An opportunity was shown, and she took it. The girl launched herself onto the monster's back, hitting it over the head again.

Millie didn't leave its back, steering the bat as she struck, into its brain, its memories, its anger. The monster screeched in pain, instinctively yanking Millie from the vulnerable position she put it in. Her body was thrown against the wall, still clutching the bat in her hand. Millie groaned in her own frustration, but she didn't let that take control of her; her only wonder was where that fleshy noise was coming from.

Its remaining human blood sat still on its head from the attack, dripping like the wound was open.

"Why did you do this to yourself?"

The monster stopped dead in its tracks, seeming to understand the words coming out of Millie's mouth. It didn't respond in any way; it just stood there, staring into her eyes.

"I know you hear me, Mr. Larson!" Millie shouted, remembering the name he was once named after.

The monster lifted its head farther back; a growl rumbling from its teeth, a snarl of hatred at that name, of what it once was. The weak, pathetic human it used to be.

# Chapter Fifteen
The Beginning of Chaos

*T*he hall was quiet, silent, the very thing he had been waiting for. The perfect time to strike, to start this slaughter that was carefully planned and considered, but there was no consideration. There was no decision.

Mr. Larson pulled out the keycard to the room, the room where all of this would begin. The pad clicked to green, unlocking the door immediately as it slid open. He crept inside, checking his surroundings before entering. This was it, a moment he had waited for, for so long, and now it was here; now it was time. He could finally murder every one of these fools; these children, their lives ended now.

Experiment One sprinted, sprinted as fast as her legs could carry her; no one knew why she was in a hurry, and it was her last mistake to not tell them.

The door burst open at floor thirty-nine. She heard the sound of footsteps across the hallways, and into that room. The girl didn't waste a second before bolting down the long angles. Scientists rolled past, not daring to stop her, for they were no match for her, no match for the mysterious power that was not given to her by them. The mysterious power they had no clue of the past of. No one was monitoring the substance; it was the time he would strike, where Mr. Larson would start his wrath.

The door stood ahead, completely opened, with no one guarding it. The security that was supposed to be there was out on their lunch break. Outside somewhere, somewhere the kids these cruel people had locked inside had no access to. She picked up her pace, her breathing heavy with each drop of sweat that ran down her face. The door swung open the last remaining inches it hadn't gone before.

Mr. Larson stood over the pit of the green liquid; she couldn't see his face, but Experiment One knew a grin was plastered over it.

*"You want to be the first to die? How relieving, I always wanted to rip out your throat," he chuckled, turning to face the girl. Her assumption was right; a sick slim smile was over his face.*

*"You're this hungry for power? That you want to wreck the lives of possibly thousands inside of this lab?" The growl was released from her throat as she took a step forward, but she didn't go any further. If she ran, she would only witness him fall in. "Why? There are children here. Children who have already had their lives ruined. Their childhoods were stolen from them. And you're just going to break them even more?"*

*She never understood his intentions, Experiment One knew he was aware of the power the children in the lab possessed, the 'lab rats' that were taken from homes that didn't want them anymore, at least that's possibly what he thought of them. But she never knew why he could be this sick, this insane, to want to ruin the lives of children that had nothing more left to take from them.*

*A smile remained on his face, a sick smile, a smile only wanting death and blood.*

*"It's a simple question, Mr. Larson." He still didn't open his mouth. "Why?" She was out of breath; the question was now a plea, a plea that needed to be answered.*

*"I so hope to see you beg for death, Experiment One."*

*Their conversation was stopped by another scientist coming in from all the shouting. The clipboard that was being held tightly in her arms dropped to the floor.*

*"Run," Experiment One ordered.*

*The scientist stood still, looking at her like she was crazy.*

*"Do you have any idea what that substance does?" she asked like the Experiment was out of her mind.*

*"Yes, I know, just go." Gene mutation, it could transform anyone into anything fate pleased.*

*The scientist left her alone with Mr. Larson again.*

*Soon alarms blared, flashing red against her vision, but she didn't even blink.*

*"Let's see who's stronger," Mr. Larson said one last time, taking a step back into the pit of green that bubbled like lava and fire. She tried to bolt, tried to stop him, but only saw the smoke rising from the tub. Guards soon rushed in but were only able to back away in confusion and fear of what they thought and prayed hadn't happened.*

*A moment of silence awaited them, along with Experiment One who could only stand there in confusion of what to do next; she thought of taking out her sword, but she didn't need it just yet, not until a couple of seconds later this time.*

*A black claw emerged at the front of the giant bowl, then a splash came, another claw appearing afterwards.*

*White beamy eyes shot out from the fluid, a humanoid black body accompanying them.*

*"Fire!" a guard yelled, guns went into the air, and bullets came with them. All she could do was duck and take cover.*

*The thing that used to be Mr. Larson, charged right for them. A splatter of red created layers throughout the floor; a second cover went on top of it. Before she could even realize the sound of the blaring red lights, everyone that had been assigned to attack was dead before her. Not a single bullet had hit; it had dodged them all. Now it was staring directly at her, standing over a dead guard that had seemed to try and use a melee weapon on it. The Experiment could only guess what used to be Mr. Larson had called it a fool from his mind. Mr. Larson was no longer a human; it had reincarnated through its own body, and had become death incarnate.*

*Her blue sword faded into her hand, a bright light pulsing through it. The blade was held in her fingers as she moved it to face the beast's heart, like a knight fighting a dragon. This is what she was here for, and she would stand against it with one mission: protect them all.*

*The thing lunged, stretching out those now red infested claws. The girl sliced the elbow in a quick movement, so fast the monster couldn't even process it for a moment, slamming into the ground while closing its eyes as it grunted in pain. Once it opened them, the sword was waiting for it.*

*It was able to roll out of the way before the blade was jammed into its throat. The quick movement had probably saved its life, and to its excitement, caused the girl to miss and forced the sword into the ground instead. Experiment One felt her heart drop. This was the first time ever, she had realized what fear of death felt like, not for herself, but for those children.*

*A slash went across her cheek, warming it with her own hot blood. Experiment One couldn't stop herself from rolling, couldn't stop the movement that made her so defenseless, so vulnerable. She tumbled back, falling as far away from her sword as she possibly could, perfectly what it wanted.*

*It ran, ran as fast as it had killed those men. Those men who had once been partners, partners that he had envied deep inside, who he now had slaughtered them in cold blood. The beast went flying through the air once it made it a few feet away from the child he deemed way wiser than someone who lived a short life. Raising its claw, the monster stared deep into her eyes before it struck what might have been its final attack, but it hadn't. It didn't know what happened after that. That was all it could remember, those eyes full of fear, but determination.*

***

"Power was more important than your good life?" It snapped back to reality, was only able to stand there, leaned over to avoid hitting the ceiling over its head, staring at her, its teeth hidden in its mouth.

"Why would you abandon everything you had?" Millie shouted, taking a step closer to its position.

The monster growled in response, her words irritating it in a personal way. "What about your family? Your friends! Everyone around you—"

The monster jumped at her, its anger taking full control of its decisions. Millie tried to leap to the side again, but the monster yanked her back, slamming her into the floor. It held her neck and squeezed it tight, attempting to choke her to death like the first time they had met, after a long while at least. Millie gripped the hand that was holding her in her situation, squeezing it tight.

The monster growled in the sharp pain from her recent hits, raising its hand in the air, and scratching her deep dark blood across her forehead. It watched as the red fluid ran down her face, making the fatal injury look way worse than it already was. She didn't flinch with the pain; she wasn't going to give this thing a reaction. What she said really angered it, and all it wanted now was for her to suffer. Good, exactly what she needed.

The monster squeezed her throat tighter and lifted her head, then it slammed her further into the stone. Her pupils dilated, blood jerked out of her nose; the convulsions kicked in, shaking her muscles violently while they contracted. Now her head decided to finally give in to something it had refused to do before, something she had controlled before. She wouldn't let herself fall; she wouldn't let her consciousness leave her, not now. She needed to help her friends; she couldn't let them down, not like the others.

"Your anger controls you," Millie said, struggling to even say the words. "That will lead to your downfall."

Instead of the painful injuries she had given the monster during her previous encounters, her fist speared its stomach, right into the most fatal spot, the heart. She put her arm further into its chest. Flesh contorted and shattered under the weight of her strength. Blood covered her fingers and stained her skin red. The monster screamed in pain, finally snapping back to reality from the wrath that stormed through its now hurt heart. In retaliation, it stabbed her directly through her chest with its own claws. The monster couldn't focus on the short fight much longer, as it stumbled from Millie, holding its chest in its pain. The injury wouldn't kill it, the regeneration it held would save it, but it gave the kids enough time to run far away and get out of the building. Millie knew they would make it.

She couldn't get up at first, due to the wound in her chest that missed her pounding heart by an inch. She was soon able to stand on her feet, but the convulsions still zoomed through her body, making it hard to stand up fully. She fought through it, the unimaginable pain of the built-up injuries she had received throughout this mission, this death sentence she knew might come. Her body could take more than the others. That's what the lab had found out. A foot was placed in front of her, her own foot, blood fell into her mouth, but she didn't care about the taste. That wasn't something to think about at that moment. Millie kept moving forward, until she reached a hallway from that room, placing a hand on the filthy stone wall, so she could give herself a chance to turn and face the monster that was still squealing in pain on the floor.

"It will lead to your downfall," she repeated, leaving the monster to do its thing.

Their freedom mattered more than the monster's death, and she couldn't fight anymore. It would help; the monster's regeneration could buy them some time. It afforded them it, and she hoped it would profit. Millie turned away into the hallway, leaving the monster for God to decide what will happen. Millie activated her healing power; she would have to find some bandages. The injuries she had would not benefit her in a good way on the rest of the journey, and the healing power might not keep her alive if she passed out.

Mitchell looked over at Lisa, who was walking right next to him, holding the hand of Sally. A comforting method, some way to help the poor child with her fear, to help the both of them.

"How are we going to find Millie?" he asked; the question would hopefully not rot his mind forever anymore.

"I don't know." Her response wasn't any sort of way to lie or comfort him. There wasn't really a point since Mitchell wasn't the type to try and follow through a fake, comforting lie.

Mitchell didn't know why he asked the question, but he did it anyway for a reason he had no knowledge of.

"Should we go back?" Charlie suggested, bumping into the conversation at the start of the group.

"But what if the monster's still there?" Sally said as she quivered at the thought of it. She wanted to know if Millie was alright, but that thing haunted her head and would forever.

A bang was heard behind them, almost sounding like a gun, but it sounded softer. Soon they saw what it was.

Millie came tumbling around the corner with a giant bloody hole on the side of her chest, coughing out half of her bloodline. Charlie was the first to bolt towards her, even before Lisa. Millie spit out more red blood, losing a step of her feet, tipping over, and falling to the floor. Sally watched her friend suffering with tears in her eyes.

"Do we have a clean cloth or something?" Lisa asked in a shout of panic.

"There is a hole in her chest! I think we're going to need more than a clean cloth!" Michael barked in his panicking, gesturing to the giant wound in Millie's chest with both of his hands.

They rushed over to Millie; Micheal placed his hands on the wound in hopes to stop the blood. Charlie had tears bubbling in her eyes.

*Oh no. No, no.*


Millie awoke on something soft, not something common in the lab, now that it was destroyed. The texture gave her the obvious clue that it was a mattress.

She lifted her head, just to see the wound in her chest was gone, no bandage, only small spots of blood were on her chest, but stains were the only thing they were. No pain either, only a sore ache. She stood up straight with a confused expression, and a mind spreading with questions of confusion.

Millie exited the mattress, ignoring the ache of sleeping for so long, not knowing how long it had been since she was awake as she was examining the room around her. The lights on the ceiling were broken, but one still gave off a bright glow, which made Millie duck her head to avoid the blind it shined so brightly.

The door opened to the room, and Sally peaked through, holding the door with two arms gripping the side of it. Once she saw that Millie was awake, she jumped at her, leaping into her arms.

"She's awake!" Sally screamed in excitement and joy, wrapping her arms around Millie's chest.

They had heard the monster screaming, which must have meant Millie had damaged it badly, but not before getting a strike that almost ended her. Lisa plucked her head through when she heard the shout and was close enough, a smile going across her face. She fully emerged into the room, stopping to see Sally squeeze her tight before running and hugging Millie herself.

"Are you okay?" Lisa asked, pulling away.

"Yeah," Millie answered.

"Do you feel any symptoms? Like do you feel dizzy, like you're about to throw up, or…" Lisa paused, thinking of anything else. "Just anything like that, basically."

"I am feeling fine, why?" Millie asked, raising an eyebrow while still hugging Sally.

"Well, we sort of injected you with a syringe that said it healed any injury. It worked, but…we don't know the side effects of it." She watched Lisa scratch her head in an awkward moment.

"So, you inserted a drug into my body?"

"Yeah, that's how it went down."

Silence overflowed the room, filling it like a deep blue lake, though Millie didn't seem worried in the slightest.

"Was the liquid inside blue?" she asked.

"Yeah?"

"Then, I should be fine. That was one of the completed syringes," Millie claimed, letting go of Sally who ran out of the room to go and tell the others.

"What happened after I passed out?" Millie asked another question; Lisa looked at her with a worried look. "Sorry, just want to know."

"After you passed out, we brought you into the closest room. And we found that syringe, Charlie remembered what it did since they used it on her once…so we decided to use it on you in a panic, and it worked."

"Thank you," Millie said, hoping the rest would get the message as well.

The kids continued their journey, but the future ahead was unknown, and none of them would be prepared for it.

# Chapter Sixteen

The Final Battle for Freedom

The group had come a long way, dangerous obstacles, a ferocious monster, and they had survived it all.

The kids were brave, despite their fear. Despite the injuries, they all are still alive, and she knew they would survive until the end, not because of confidence, but of all the time they've spent together. She knew they would live. She always thought that, and always would, even in death.

The kids strolled through the large room, unaware of the danger right below them, staying quiet, none of them having something to say, except Charlie. A thought was roaming her mind; it had been for a while. She rubbed her head, trying to get rid of the thought, since she couldn't convince herself to confront Millie about it, since the girl might not even know herself, then it would be awkward. Charlie had stopped dead in her tracks.

Millie was the first to notice. "What's on your mind now?"

Charlie snapped back to her senses with those words. Finally, the thing she had been wanting to say for so long left her.

"What if you aren't able to fight the people trying to take us away? To another lab?" Millie looked at her for a moment before answering.

"I'll try, but if I'm not, it might be a life on the run." The entire group of kids now had their eyes on Millie. "But who knows? Maybe they have changed in the past years we've been stuck here."

A crinkle of stone was heard on the floor, catching everyone off guard. Charlie felt something against her foot, and she glared down at her toes.

The floor below Charlie was cracked; it rang in her ears instantly, causing the conversation to end.

"Charlie. Don't move," Millie ordered, her words changing from the original sentence. Her feet slowly walked towards Charlie, unaware if the floor around was going to break as well. The girl shook in fear, automatically activating her power, showing the fall of floors below.

"Oh no, no, no, no, no, *no,*" Charlie yelped her panicked words.

Somehow a chain of holes was carved through the floor, like a giant missile had gone right through the middle. The floor creaked its stone into more webs before Charlie could think of taking a step. Her hands were spread out at her sides, some way to keep herself from falling and splattering the unstable stone beneath her.

Millie took another step forward, giving Charlie a small piece of hope. But it was pointless. Charlie took a step like Millie did; that was her final mistake. The floor shattered; Charlie fell right through it. Millie tackled herself into the floor, reaching her hand out only for Charlie's to miss it.

"The rest of the stairs should be fine! Get to the first floor!" Millie shouted, plunging into the hole in front of her.

The rest stood in shock; they still couldn't even process what was going on, but eventually they followed her words and bolted down the stairs that were near them. They don't know her plan but trust her enough to keep Charlie and herself alive.

Charlie could see the figure of Millie falling far away from her to the point where her form was blurry, and she couldn't comprehend it at first. Charlie extended a hand, hoping Millie could get close enough to reach it. The wind passed through her, lifting her short hair into the direction of the sky. She couldn't even blink properly; the wind pressed against her only source of seeing, blocking her from resting her eyes. Millie was somehow falling faster, closer and closer she went, closer she was into grabbing Charlie's hand, the closer they were into reaching a different way to freedom, *death.* Not what they had planned at all, not what they had been fighting for; they had been fighting to see outside, and this wasn't it. They were going to die in this dark hole. It wasn't what she wanted now; it wasn't what any of them wanted. Charlie looked back at Millie, who was inches away from reaching her hand now, only being able to touch her fingertips. Charlie extended her hand further, farther than usual, to where that normal ache snapped. Millie yanked it up, pulling Charlie closer to her. The first floor drew closer, causing Millie to grab Charlie quickly and pull her in front of her as she rolled her back to face the ground. Millie was about to shield her from the fall, and there was nothing she could do to change that.

"Are you crazy?" Charlie screamed.

Millie only smiled at her before the world suddenly stopped.

Millie struck the floor, slamming into it like a meteor of fire crashing down to earth. Charlie landed on her, taking little damage by hitting Millie instead, but all she could hear was the crack of bones. The oldest felt her back shattering, her bones shaking in spider webs. Charlie crawled from Millie; her expression soon turned surprised when Millie was able to get up.

"Are you okay?" Millie asked, standing up on her feet as she looked over to Charlie, who was still on the ground; her hand was placed on her own arm. Charlie assumed she might have been using her ability again.

"Are you okay?" Charlie retorted worryingly with a shout, something everyone wanted to say to her, grabbing Millie's helping hand she had placed not that long ago.

"Yeah, I'll be okay." Her hand was placed against her back, activating the healing power again. "I should be fine...did you break anything though?"

"Millie. I appreciate your concern, but you just fell—"

"We."

"Well, it looks like we just fell ten stories–or more even! How did those even get there anyway—"

***

*It felt like the world had just stopped, like time had ended out of nowhere. Charlie looked around, only to see a scientist stroll right through her body. She jumped back at the scare, tripping into the ground of cold stone. The kid opened her eyes again; another scientist walked past her, as if she wasn't there. Charlie never was there, not at this time; kids were never allowed out of their rooms without assistance. It was still the first floor, but way back then.*

*What was this, a memory? A flash of the past?*

*It certainly looked like it; the place looked brand new, cleaned to the core of the stone walls that were now ruined with moss and rotten dried blood. Scientists wandered everywhere; one had a kid cuffed while he held her hand. A bruise banged on her cheek, possibly a punch from resisting. She hated the sight of it, her cold lifeless eyes that were holding on by a thread.*

*There was a scream, a sudden scream of fear, and pain.*

*Then there was running, footsteps clattered down the stairs, one bigger, one smaller. The door busted open, and a mangled body fell right out of it.*

*The man looked up at the scientists: the last remains; his eyes darkened by the blood and guts over his face.*

*His eye sockets vanished as they closed, and as a humanoid tall figure's shadow casted over the room.*

*Screaming erupted, so loud that it covered the red blaring alarms that went off too late. Charlie couldn't move, she didn't know what to do, what to think, or how to react.*

*The monster started the beginning of the last kills, swiping and biting, thrashing and stabbing every last person it saw.*

*The girl was one of the second to be slashed; blood was yanked from her body as she fell lifeless to the ground, a limp body with a soul that was already gone. There was a ringing in her ear, a pitched squeal that screamed at her to run.*

*The room exploded into a blue light, blinding. Instinctively, Charlie closed her eyes, covering them into darkness to avoid the sting of the flash.*

*And then they opened once that light faded, and all Charlie could see was a giant sword piercing down the monster's stomach, coming from thousands of holes created in the ceiling.*

***

It disappeared; the world went back to normal, and she was standing before Millie, a hand on her shoulder. Millie jumped back, her fingers shaking while her eyes looked at them with shock.

"What was that?" Charlie asked.

Millie silently shrugged with her head shaking; her eyes widened with confusion.

"Millie, did you...?" Charlie's question was followed by a growl, a growl from neither of them.

The girl froze; Millie whipped at where Charlie stared in terror.

There stood the monster, looking for revenge it had been craving for so long, for a time that was like eternity.

"Run," was all Millie could say.

Charlie didn't hesitate to bolt from the whisper of Millie, who followed behind her instantly, but she was yanked before the two could reach a hallway. Charlie looked back; Millie was being dragged by the monster.

"Oh no, you are not doing this again!" Charlie snarled, sprinting back to Millie.

"Charlie, stay back!" her oldest friend ordered.

Charlie didn't stop. She yanked a sharp stone from the ground, aiming for the knee of the monster who didn't have time to react by the time it noticed. It growled as it backed off.

"You just fell more than ten floors! I'm not leaving you to fight this thing when you are injured! Not again!" she argued, standing by Millie's side as she helped her friend lift herself to her feet, her legs wobbling and trembling. It watched them argue in amusement while tapping its feet and hands silently. Impatiently waiting for them to start this battle it so eagerly craved.

"You promised, Millie."

"I..." Millie didn't have time to say something back before the thing lunged at her, its mouth baring its vampire-like fangs.

In instinct, she pushed Charlie out of the way as the thing shoved her to the ground and prepared to strike its claws.

Charlie jumped onto its back, clenching the end of a broken broomstick in her fingers. The monster's claws reached for her neck, her throat, any type of grip. She ducked out of the way as it started to spin in a circle. Charlie shanked the weapon made to clean into the blood-soaked skin of the neck. The monster tried to use that as a chance to get her off, but the kid wasn't done; she wanted blood. Charlie ripped it out; red dripped from the sharp tip. The girl didn't hesitate to shank it again, piercing the head this time. The monster screamed in pain as it felt the wound beating it like a knife to the throat over and over again. The thing started twirling and twisting in an attempt to pull her off. The witness to the battle would have thought he might have been ballerina dancing, jumping through the air and landing perfectly on his feet, reaching its arm behind its head. Charlie held on strong as she dodged, piercing again and again, straight into the head repeatedly, red splattering onto the cold stone underneath their feet.

Charlie flinched at the claws holding her leg, squeezing them tight with its claws. Blood spilled as it tossed her aside through the air. Her back crashed into the hard rock floor, an aching pain soaring through her skin. The monster was bolting towards her.

*Get up, Get up.*

The monster tried to harm her, tried to torture her like it had done to Millie, but Charlie wanted blood, and simple stings wouldn't stop her. *She wasn't done.* Charlie leaped to the side, watching the monster plunge into the floor, missing her by a second in both of their blind rages. She wanted revenge, for her friends, for herself, for everyone that it hurt.

She took the chance, getting onto the monster's back as she held the broomstick over her head, the sharp edge facing the beast. The wood ran straight through the back of its neck, pushing and pushing it even further through. The monster thrashed its arms around, slashing Charlie across the face. Its arm squeezed her neck sooner than she expected and slammed her into the ground beside it, giving her a taste of her own. Blood leaked from her nose, falling right past her lip. But her anger boiled inside of her, and she wanted more blood, more, all of it, every last drop. The beast collapsed to the floor. It was so tired, so weak after all this running. It had forgotten that it was once human, wasn't death itself, the incarnate of the demise of humanity. Exhaustion was finally getting the best of it.

"Calm down!" Millie suddenly yelled, knowing what the outcome would be. "Use its anger against it, it can't control itself anymore!"

Her breath full of anger and frustration escaped her lips, staring at Millie like she was insane.

Charlie didn't want to listen. She didn't want to 'calm down,' but the only way to kill it would be to think, and letting her anger control her wasn't it. She took a deep breath, which didn't relieve her from the anger boiling inside of her at all. She stood on her feet, even though she struggled; she kept strong and firm. The girl clenched her fists together, which were full of her own blood, and the beast laying before her. What would be the most fatal spot? They had tried everything, the eyes, the mouth, the neck, whatever Millie had done to it beforehand; it could regenerate anything. She didn't have time to think; the monster pushed itself up with a hand. It was standing back on its two feet, a shadow looming over her, covering her whole body in its dark counterpart. Nothing could be eviler than this thing though besides the devil himself.

Charlie didn't let her fear blend her final decision. She stood her ground, ignoring the pain throughout her entire body.

*Calm down, calm down, calm down–*

The monster screamed as it swung its claw towards her face, but the girl ducked, her hand clenched into a fist as she punched it directly in the stomach, knocking it back the tiniest two inches she would ever see. A growl clogged its throat in frustration; the only reaction she would get out of it if she went physical with her attacks. It was healing its wounds, regenerating every drop of blood that wasn't able to escape.

She had to get that stick out of its neck, though it was the only other thing clogging the regeneration process. It was her only lethal weapon. She had to find some other way to kill it, some other way to bring it down for good. The monster menacingly took steps toward her, slowly creeping up on her even though she was staring directly at it.

A sledgehammer hit the thing straight across the back of its gut, its body forced into the ground.

Millie clenched the handle in her fingers. Somehow, she had spotted it randomly on the floor, help from God she supposed.

The monster let out a roar of anger, a shout of a savage beast.

Millie dropped to the floor, hitting the deck and kicking her foot into its leg in a smooth and quick swerve, despite the agony that was in her spine, despite the pain that came from this fight. The monster toppled into the ground, the aching pain from the blow still in its back. Charlie took the chance and ran over; her hands yanked the broom and tried to pull it out of its throat, but the thing wasn't falling for that again. It jumped to its feet, not sparing a moment to swipe a claw right across her face, slashing over her eye. Blood leaped from the mark. Charlie wiped some of the red goo from her soaking red face. The red puddle stayed still on her palm. There was so much of it, but it wasn't worse than the ones she had got before. Charlie was too focused on the blood, and that gave the monster a quick advantage.

The creature charged at her, preparing to strike once more. But Millie grabbed the arm and yanked it away; it wasn't getting a single chance to hurt her again. The monster tried to let loose of her grip, but Millie held it tightly, throwing it aside as hard as she could. Its slim figure toppled through the air, at least ten feet away. Charlie stared in shock for a second, before returning to the pain in her eye. She had been through worse; this was something she could deal with.

"How many more stairs are there?" Michael shouted in frustration, running after his sister with the two smaller kids.

"I don't know! Are you trying to count?" Lisa asked in her yell back, slowing down her pace to give him and the kids a bigger chance of catching up.

Michael's feet were soon running by Lisa's, along with the other two kids who were right behind.

"Are they going to be alright?" Sally yelped, raising her voice as loud as she could to get it in their ears.

"I don't know, okay? They just fell ten stories, I don't know." Lisa didn't try to lie this time, she was too worried about the question herself, and she hoped the answer was yes. She hoped so badly to the point she thought of starting prayer.

The four continued running, bolting and turning each corner of the stairwell that seemed to go on forever. The only way down was filled with rubble and holes. Anything that could get in their way was in front of them, and it wasn't going to disappear.

The monster swung, but it only tumbled into the ground, giving Charlie another chance to fight back. Once it got up, it didn't have time to defend the young girl's blow as it got punctured in the side with a dagger from the floor. She didn't know where it had come from, but it was there and she wasn't going to complain about it.

The monster tried to lunge for her, but it was rammed in the stomach by Millie, launching it back. Its feet smeared along the ground in its landing. A sneer spat at the two, some sort of intimidation display; it didn't work. It only put on a show of how frustrated it was, how angry, how pathetic. The creature's mouth opened, two sharp teeth saying it was ready to bite one of them in the throat. It wanted to so badly, it would kill all of them, every last one of them was going to die by its own hands, starting with the two-standing right in front of it.

It stared at Charlie and Millie, looking for the next move made by one of them, or perhaps it would do it itself. The broom it had thrown out of its neck was lying behind it, and it would guard it with its life, and Millie could tell. It was in a protective stance; the same one it had taken when it was guarding the generator. They would have to find some other way to stop it in its miserable life, whether it be killing it, or trapping it and letting it starve. They would end it, one way or another. The monster had always been thinking the same thing, ever since it first saw Millie. Ever since it saw her eyes, it wouldn't stop hunting like the predator it was, and it wouldn't stop until she was dead.

The monster was the first to jump, its anger wasn't containable, it wanted them dead. It wanted to see their blood spilled across the ground, splashing along its palms. Millie elbowed Charlie out of the way, her mind was swirling, she couldn't think of anything else. She had done it just in time since it had snatched her neck, forcing her into the wall. Charlie tried to sneak up on it, but the thing was too aware of their movements now.

The thing propelled her with its leg, kicking her across the room. The kid coughed dust in her mouth as she slid across the floor.

Charlie rose from the sudden attack; she wasn't done and would never be done until that thing was gone. Millie couldn't think of some way to kill it, some way to end its life. They had to get out of there; both were too critically injured to keep fighting. Millie opened her mouth wide, biting down on the thing's arm. It was so unexpected that the thing jerked back, confused on why she even thought of doing that? But the pain was too much as well. The wounds on its body seemed to irritate it, and it couldn't handle another attack, but its anger boiled deep inside of it. It told itself to go kill those kids.

Now.

# Chapter Seventeen
### Hide

Charlie looked up, only to see the thing pushed aside, and Millie running towards her. Her hand was grabbed by her friends and was whisked away before she could even process what was going on. Blood was dripping from both of their noses; she could feel a shake from Millie's body in the contact of their hands. The monster screamed in the distance behind them, faded, and a long way from them.

"What are you doing?" Charlie whispered, following Millie as they ran around the corner. Darkness consumed them; dim lights flickered above their heads as they tried to get as far away as they could.

"We are too injured. We have to think of some other way to kill it, but we can't do that if it's about to kill us itself," Millie explained the best way she could without choking on her own blood.

The girl opened the nearest door quickly, running inside while dragging Charlie along with her. The room was dark, but Charlie could still hear the door shut behind them. She could feel Millie crouching down, so she slid down along with her. Charlie didn't dare say a word, not when they were trying to hide from this thing. But it could see through walls; how were they supposed to hide?

"The thing can see through walls," Charlie whispered with a slight hint of annoyance, anxiously squirming her eyes around in the dark. "It's going to see us, Millie."

"Not if it's dark," Millie claimed.

"It's going to be obvious if one specific room is dark."

"A lot of these rooms are dark, Charlie."

Oh, yeah, she forgot about that. Crunching footsteps were heard down the hallway; it shut both up fast, which made Charlie tug Millie's hand tighter, and she didn't even realize it. It was her fear controlling her, and she wouldn't let it; she soothed her muscles, lowering the sound of her loud breathing.

A growl was heard close to their door, but it didn't sound like it was outside. Charlie slowly lifted her eyes to the roof. Once they reached their target, her dark green eyes widened with horror. Glowing white eyes stared directly back at her. Saliva wept from its teeth, ready to devour both of them.

The door was suddenly opened, and her body was hauled out of it. The two were now sprinting down a bright hallway faster than that thing could run. Though they spent little time in a dark room, their eyes were acting like they had just taken a long nap in the shadows. The monster jumped out of the pitch-black space, staying on the ceiling like a spider, and bolting after them right over their heads. Millie still didn't let go of Charlie's hand; she seemed to notice how weak Charlie was getting, and she was right. She had used her power so much: she couldn't really run anymore. Charlie had tried to ignore the exhaustion, had tried to ignore the urge to fall, but it was too powerful. She almost stumbled, but she kept herself going, though eventually she was going to stop, and that sight wasn't going to look pretty.

Lisa slammed herself into the door; it was jammed by something. She ran into it again, it still wouldn't budge.

"It's being held by something," she said in frustration, turning away as if ignoring the door will make it magically disappear.

"Is it the monster?" Sally asked, putting her fists together by her mouth in fear.

"I hope not, but probably no," Michael said, trotting over to his sister to help her. He searched the area; all he saw was a code panel.

"It's an operated door, Lisa. It requires a code to open," Michael explained, hitting the code panel to clarify his statement.

"Oh, okay, do you have any idea what the code could be?" Lisa asked, since her brother knew more about mechanics, even though that wouldn't have anything to do with the code.

Michael stroked his chin with his thumb; it somehow irritated Lisa, who was entirely stressed at the moment.

"That's not going to help your thinking," Lisa snarled, her lips quivering in fear for Charlie and Millie.

"Well, this place was created…" He typed his thought into the panel, pressing enter right afterwards. Despite his calm composure, he was terrified too. The panel beeped.

Lisa yanked the doorknob immediately when she heard it. It didn't open. Michael thought of the owner of the place; he thought of all the information. He tried the birth first. It beeped, but it didn't open. The owner had died before the place was completed, so he tried the death date. It didn't open.

"I have no other ideas left," he sighed in his failure.

"What if we try to break it?" Lisa suggested. "Maybe it would open then?"

"I could try and break it?" Mitchell stepped in, raising his hand as if his politeness mattered right now.

"But wouldn't that exhaust you?" Michael recalled the last time he had used it.

"That doesn't matter," Mitchell argued, passing through Michael and Lisa and right in front of the box.

"Can you move...farther away?" Mitchell pleaded, opening the door to the fuse box. Already he could feel the electricity inside, like it was ready for him. He placed his hand inside; the electric currents were burning hot, but he fought through the pain. Even though the urge to let go was so high, he fought back. The flowing blue spikes of the electrical currents attached themselves to him. He could feel the heat building up inside of him, the intense fire hit him like the deepest part of the torturing world below. He fought through it, for the sake of his friends, two that had saved his life many times.

"Are you doing alright?" Lisa yelled from their spot on the stairs, holding Sally behind her arm, who stared at her friend with deep concern.

Mitchell tried to speak; he tried so hard, but all that came out was grunts of pain. The electricity zoomed faster through the box, bouncing off the walls faster than lightning itself.

His mouth opened as the collected energy burst inside of his body, traveling down his hands, and flying right back into the fuse box.

Mitchell flew back as the box erupted in a fiery explosion, landing right on his head. He heard footsteps running down the stairs, and the click of a door opening. It worked, it had *actually worked*. A smile went across his face, even though his body still hurt with an aching pain, a pain full of fire, but it worked; his body had conducted it like last time, and the door had opened. It worked; *it had actually worked.*

Millie stopped at the dead end of the hallway, letting go of Charlie's hand. They both stared at it, like it was their death. Ironically, it was.

"Oh come on..." Charlie muttered, slowly turning her head to the hallway they had just run through.

The monster crawled on all fours at the end, scraping its front claw against the hard man-made floor. Millie stood in front of Charlie, spreading her arm out in front of her, of course she did. What did Charlie expect? The monster slowly inched closer, taking its sweet old time even though it knew fully that Charlie could run through walls like it did, but it didn't care that much about Charlie; it wanted Millie.

"Go," Millie ordered, not giving a full context of what she meant.

"What?" Charlie's eyebrows shot up.

"Go, go through the wall and run."

"Break the wall and come with me then!"

"I can't, I'll probably pass out!"

"Then, I am not leaving you again," Charlie retorted.

"You will have to if you want to live!"

"If we die, then we die together. That's that!"

Millie knew there was no way in convincing Charlie. She sighed in fear, going back to face the death that lay ahead of them. The monster elevated, standing on its two feet once again. It continued its menacing move, taking one step at a time, an intimidation tactic. And it was working, traversing through the rubble and stones ahead, kicking them aside or tossing them entirely. Either way, it was going to reach them, no matter the cost.

A rock pummeled it in the head unexpectedly, rocking its head to the right. The monster whipped around.

Lisa was standing at the end; another piece of ammo held in her hand, her brother and her other friends behind him.

The beast growled, showing its teeth as it changed its plans. The main goal was forgotten, which was to kill Millie, but its anger had taken a toll, and that plan was washed away in its frustration.

It screamed, going into a gallop as it jumped onto all fours once again. Lisa and the others backed away in fear. Millie didn't expect the plan to go like this; she knew they were there. She was only distracting it to give them time, but she didn't know it was going to run at them. She had forgotten it was too full of its anger now to even care about the main focus. Millie wanted to scold herself for that one but now was not the time at all.

Millie looked to Charlie, who was gone again. She wanted to whip around anxiously for her, but she knew what her friend was up to.

The monster leaped through the air, planning to rip one of them apart, but a knife wielded by Charlie went through its head. Blood squirted in her face when she struck with a second knife, sending the monster to the floor with two knives sticking out of its body. Charlie had surprised it; she had jumped through the wall and followed it, finding two knives in a room on her way. She sliced her feet on the stone floor as she landed.

The plan had worked perfectly, right to the exact detail. Charlie felt like thanking God for that one, but she was pulled away by Millie.

She looked back on the monster that she had slaughtered, or wished she had done.


The group ran with every last ounce of strength in their legs; they had come a long way, and this was it. This was the final floor, the final showdown. The kids reached the end of the hallway.

A red door was at the end. A sign overhead that read 'exit' was waiting for them. It was as beautiful as they imagined it, as welcoming as they wanted it to be.

Millie gestured to them with her hand, but they didn't need a gesture, all they needed was their motivation to freedom, but that happiness was soon stopped.

The monster plummeted to the ground before them, not even landing on its two feet. It was too desperate to murder them all in cold blood, not a care in the world; it wanted them all dead. It didn't want them breathing for much longer.

"Are you kidding—"

The monster ran straight at Millie, opening its jaw to show the teeth that had murdered thousands. Millie didn't try and move out of the way; it would only put the lives of the others in danger. So, she stood her ground, only to be slammed into the rest. All the kids were knocked over into solid ground. Charlie got up first, lunging at the savage beast with a rock that she picked up just beforehand. It was stupid, but she was too anxious to try and think of an ulterior plan. The monster was too focused on Millie to deflect Charlie's swipe of the rock.

It bashed it straight in the head. The monster attempted to swing its claw in retaliation, but its blow didn't hit a single thing. The creature steadied itself to prevent its body from falling, somehow being considerate for once. It wiped the blood dripping from its mouth, looking back at the group of frightened children, scanning each one of them, as if it was looking for a new target. The eyes of the man-slaughtering monster stopped on Millie; its goal was set and had been set for a while. Its claws thrashed as it bounced at Millie. The girl was ready to take another hit, but she only saw a lighting flash before her eyes as Mitchell stuck onto the things back, electrocuting it with the electricity he had stolen from a nearby fuse. Blue flashed in the air, as the monster screamed along with Mitchell.

The monster threw him off fast. He collided into the floor behind Sally, who was still frozen, not knowing what to do. The monster focused its attention on the child, who was getting in the way between it and Mitchell.

It roared at her, taking advantage of her improved senses that it had actually worked on with other scientists.

Sally covered her ears, tears falling down her face with the amount of pain she was in as she stumbled back, wanting to run, wanting to scream back at it. But the pain was too much. The monster bolted for her, preparing to take her out first. But it didn't expect Millie to wrap around its neck, distracting it from hurting the youngest. The monster struggled to get the girl off, like Charlie had done before, exactly what they wanted.

"Hey!" It heard the voice of one of the oldest, which made it zip in the direction of her position, only to meet the blinding flash of her eyes. Millie closed hers just in time. It screamed while covering its face in the pain of such a blinding light. In desperation, the monster threw itself against the nearest wall, ramming Millie into the stone headfirst. Millie's muscles gave out on her, forcing her to rest on the ground. She pushed her muscles harder, yelling at them to get up, but she was unable to. She watched as the monster went to the closest person, Michael.

"Oh no—" the boy gasped as he tried to run, but he was only cornered instead; his words stopped instantly. His fear took over his actions, his thoughts on how to get out of this situation. It came closer, closer and closer until it was a few feet away.

He punted the thing right in the stomach as he activated his power, sending the thing flying across the room. Nothing could stop it. It couldn't cling onto something to save it. The tall humanoid figure crashed into the stone sealing it in the jail cell it had created.

The kick seemed to irritate it, since it didn't hesitate to run back to him; the hurtful itches were ignored on its body. Michael sprinted to his left to escape its plunge. The tall figure yanked his arm instead, stopping his escape, gripping it tight as it chucked him into the floor. Lisa ran for it, attempting to blind it again, but the weird position of the monster stopped her in her tracks. The thing scratched its head, digging into its own blood wounds. Lisa felt mucus rising in her throat at the sight of it, hearing a fleshy nose in its head, like something was moving inside.

She pressed her hands against her lips, her eyes widening with horror. Horns grew out of the monster's head, revealing a glowing aura underneath. Blood dripped from the holes it had created itself. Michael scooted away on his bum, too in shock and fear to try and get up. The monster curved the upper part of its mouth, a smile, a sick one, rotating its eyes. The reflection of Michael inside of them peered back at it. Michael moved further away, but the thing was faster on two feet, and soon it was standing over him, with pure killing intent. It heard Lisa charging it from behind, it only had to extend a claw, and Lisa fell right into its grasp. It hurled her away and heard her slam into the wall. It didn't even have to look. It only stared into Michael's eyes, knowing it would be the last thing he would see before his gruesome death. Lifting a claw, the beast reached the sharp points towards Michael's face, the tips approached the kid's eyes, it wanted this death to be slow and painful.

It let out a quiet yelp, a silent shriek of pain. Michael could tell where it was coming from. A blue tip was piercing right through the thing's chest, glowing with a peaceful aura.

A sign of hope, a sign of victory. The blue tip speared further into the thing's chest, revealing itself to be a sword, moving the thing closer to Michael, but it was soon pulling the beast back and into the air. It held it in place, and through that body of death, the main killer of this place. He saw someone else, someone he had known for so long, Millie.

The protector of this place, finishing what it started.

# Chapter Eighteen

The Loss of Two Beings

Her eyes were glowing with a beautiful light blue, like she had come directly from heaven, from the stars above and beyond that, beyond this world, or the universe itself. The group around them was in absolute disbelief; they couldn't even think. Millie said she couldn't use it, or it would kill her.

"Run…now," Millie ordered it as a whisper, not like her other orders.

"Millie!" Charlie shouted, bolting for her friend. Two arms locked around her as she was pulled back. Lisa thought of letting her go; tears rolled down her face. She and Millie stared at each other, she saw the glistening light of the water in her friends' eyes.

"Run!" Her friends still refused. Millie sighed and looked at Charlie. "I'm sorry…but I can't let any of you die."

She whipped the sword; the weapon slid out of the monster's body with beautiful grace through that simple swing, and the thing crashed into the roof. Rocks rumbled and tumbled to the ground, right between their path of getting back to their friend. Dust flew into their faces, blocking their view of Millie and the beast.

"Millie!" Charlie shouted again, running for her, but the rocks shielded the fight from them. The despair, the horror. They looked at the rocks as if they were transparent. The kids hesitated, due to their utter shock still filling their minds.

"We can find another way around. Come on!" Lisa ordered, running down the hall.

They left Millie to the battlefield, hoping to make it back on time. If not, only one would be in their sights alive. But on her way, Charlie heard something out of Millie's mouth, through the rocks, in the fight.

"This ends here, Mr. Larson."

Mr. Larson? It was him, the man who turned into the beast. Whatever happened. However he mutated into the vicious monster he was now, she didn't want to know what the man had done to himself.

"I warned you, didn't I?" Millie said, watching the thing hurl itself to the ground, shaking its head, seeming to be in a daze of whirls. Its eyes darted back at Millie, who was still holding the giant blue sword at her side, letting out a growl as it stood back on all fours.

The beast snarled in response, starting to circle the young girl.

"You have killed enough people; I won't let you add to it."

The monster moved a step forward, making a low rumbling gurgle in its throat. Millie took a step as well; no smile spread across her face.

"You haven't been scaring me since the first day we met, do you think now would be the time?" She lifted the sword, starting to spin it in the air with one hand. A warmup, before this final, brutal fight.

Millie then lowered the sword, stopping it by her side, ending the spinning with just the touch of her finger.

A blue light flashed the room, a glow brighter than the ones of Lisa. Through that light, large wings emerged from Millie's back. Blood tore out of her skin, as feathers protruded from her body. She hid the pain and grimace in her face, as she narrowed her gaze at the beast before her: widened eyes and gnashing teeth.

Angelic blue feathers flapped, but she didn't fly. She only stood on her two feet, not an inch moved, seeming to not want to be the first to attack. She wasn't here for blood; she was here to protect, the oath would not falter. Eyes blinked open within the feathers, white and glowing as Lisa's did when she used her own powers. Yet these were something much bigger, much more powerful than any of them could comprehend. The blue light faded, and her now brand-new wings stood at her back, ready to fight in this body.

One last time.

The monster galloped at her, with everything it had, with that rage and anger flooding its body like a tsunami. Millie didn't dare move; she held the contact of the glowing white eyes as it came closer. Its teeth snarling exciting threats she couldn't understand.

The thing lunged into the air; the wind passed through its shiny, white sharp teeth that raised in joy.

The sword swung, and blood splattered from the sliced off tooth.

It screamed as it crashed into the floor, its claws scrambling over its mouth to hold its pain. Its torment, just like how the children felt, all of them.

Millie stood behind, straightening her sword and simply watching its agony, its cries of anger. She felt nothing for it; her eyes had no sense of sympathy or anything that would have an ounce of pity. She had tried, many times, but there was no saving it from this. There wouldn't be a point anyways.

She took a few steps back, to give it space while it rose to its feet. Her wings flapped against the soft wind. The shadows rose over the beast, higher than it would ever reach.

Its head swerved faster than she could react, and its claws swiped right to her neck. She saw her blood squirt before her very eyes, the red fluttering in the air until it splattered on the stone below her. Millie looked up, her eyes meeting a second claw that slashed her cheek, a few eyelashes cutting off and vanishing into the rocks underneath.

Millie raised the sword and its claws wrapped around the blade, meeting the blue glowing steel instead of her chest. It pushed harder and harder, her feet scraping against the floor, blood bleeding from her bare toes. A sick smile went over its face, one from the man inside, from a man that was never a human the minute he stepped foot in a torture chamber as the torturer.

Millie slapped her foot over its knee, the beast's legs buckling as its teeth clamped down on her arm, a stinging pain rising through her from the dripping red. She tore the sword under the neck, and a cut formed from the black skin. It stared at her with resentment from its excitement, and anger boiled beneath its eyes.

She expected it all, not a change of heart from him.

Its claws still crushed the steel of the blade; both their bodies shook from the struggle of the collision. She had to do something; the two weren't going to be here forever.

A hand let go of the hilt, changing into a fist and slamming into the thing's jaw. Spit was tossed from its tongue, its body bouncing from the ground with the stone from the impact of her strength. Millie gripped the sword with all her might and let it fly over her shoulder, her body tensing up from the energy that was slowly dying.

The beast stared up at the blade plummeting down into its neck. The steel tore through its skin like paper, softer and easily through the blood that sprang from its throat.

Yet, the blade stopped. Her fingers crunched against the rough hilt, but the claws around the blade were somehow more determined. The thing grinned again, again like before, again like forever.

Sounds of flesh moving with the blade swished as it pulled the sword out faster than she could push it in, and she was flung back before she knew it. Millie was on the ground; she couldn't even process it. The things glowing horns pulsed through its own shadow; her hands moved for the blade, but a scream erupted from her throat instead when her bone shattered as the monster's foot plunged down onto her arm.

It yanked her by the leg, and her body was smashed into the stone. Her forehead roared with her. The drum inside it pounded, like courage that yelled at her to get up off the ground, yearned for her to run, fight, and do anything to survive.

A harsh foot landed on her back. A rib that couldn't take the sudden hit broke within her body. Millie folded her hand into a fist against the floor, pieces of a rock swarming out of her fingers. Her heart felt like it had stopped pumping, but she knew herself that she was not done.

Millie's hand found its way to the monster's leg, and she mashed its skin, until she heard the same sound her leg and back had done. Its voice was like an explosion in her ears, its teeth jagged and preparing to strike.

She rolled out from its foot, the toes piercing her back in a heinous act. Millie fell onto her back, her eyes opening to a claw, lunging for her face. She launched her hands and gripped it mere inches away from the tip of her nose.

Her hands wrapped around the slim fingers of the beast, a deep breath blowing out of her throat. She forced its fingers apart more than humanly possible, pulled them away until blood spewed, and bones cracked. She could see the white in its horrid flesh. Its mouth opened, and a roar mightier than a lion spit onto her face, yet a scream more cowardly than a goat was what she heard. It pushed harder than it had before; its remaining claws inching closer until one touched the skin of her nose. Millie turned her eyes away, her teeth clenched, blood swimming to the side of her mouth. Her other foot started to kick, waving around like a vicious animal that had a mind of its own. Its eyes stared at her own, like a demon in the corner of a bedroom, watching, waiting for her to make one mistake, and taking her life as the cause.

Its teeth smiled at her as a grin, a cruel joy that was happy to end another life, the one that it craved to kill from the beginning. The blood leaked from the spaces of its hand; there wasn't a single twitch or even a flinch of the pain from the monster.

Rage was one of a kind drug.

Its other arm came crashing down towards her, she didn't have time to react when the finger pierced into her eyeball. She screamed; she couldn't stop herself from screaming or halting the blood that splattered onto her open tongue, or the red that stained her teeth. The finger wiggled, squirming through the red that was pouring out of her socket.

*Pain,* she hated the mere existence of it.

Millie squeezed the hand tighter; the remaining intact bones of it blew to smithereens. Her leg crashed down onto the floor; the stone shrunk larger until it looked like a meteor had landed on her foot. The impact tossed the monster back, its finger freeing itself from her eye. She grasped over it, coughing and tears forming in one of her eyes. Blood poured from her face, but the puddle beneath her was all blurry and something she could barely process.

The kids ran with everything they had, lost in the endless maze of corridors and hallways.

"What do we do?" Charlie threw a question at Lisa, who was now the temporary leader of the group.

"Look for another way around."

"Do you know another way around? Where are we even going?"

"I don't know, okay? Charlie, I'm trying!" Lisa shouted back.

Charlie stopped in her tracks, activating her power once more. The walls turned transparent, and she searched the whole area. On her way, she saw a cruel sight. The monster, holding Millie up in the air by the throat. Her friend kicked and gasped, clawing at the monster's hand. Beautiful wings dispersed from her back, and behind them? Another hallway, one they could get to her. She didn't care about the wings, didn't know where they came from, all she saw was Millie in danger.

"This way!" Charlie ran past Lisa, who followed her along with the rest.

Millie's legs kicked back and forth; her breath sounded hoarser the longer it held her up by the throat in the air. Her skin bled from everything it had done to her, to her body and soul.

Her fingers clawed at its own; it wasn't letting go. Her nails did nothing but break with blood in her attempts to be free. Her feet went into its slim stomach over and over again, but it didn't even flinch. Her heart dropped with terror; her mind froze with zero ideas of what to do next.

At least her friends weren't dead.

It threw her like a baseball, her body landing straight into a wall. The stone crumbled with the bones of her wings as she fell. Blood stained the blue feathers, the glowing pulse that flickered in her heart. She couldn't give up, she couldn't–

It was on her in moments; she didn't even get a chance to breathe. Its claws found the edge of her wings, the feathers broke under the weight. One hand was around her neck; the other started to pull.

She screamed as loud as she could, but it didn't stop the blood that leaked out of her back, the red that fell from her body when she saw her wing being tossed across the room. Her bones were ripped apart, what remained of them anyway. Her mind became dazed; her body turned weak. Her breath was nothing more than heavy smoke that damaged everything.

Millie didn't try to save her other wing, her last remaining feathers that floated into the puddle of blood around her as they were torn from her back. The beast's eyes were the only thing she saw in the blur, the only glow she could watch. She hated that.

She couldn't fight for that much longer; it would only be a matter of time when her body would shut down before the thing could do it itself. Maybe that would be a type of justice against it.

Millie rolled her head over; her eye caught the sight of her blade, out of reach, but still glowing, alive. It wasn't that much of an object, but something to be summoned whenever she pleased.

Her fingers widened; her bleeding skin tore even further from the cuts and scratches that had formed. She glared at the beast with her one open eye; it was too focused on her to notice her fingers. Good, let it be that way.

The sword started to vanish; the blue sparkling lights quivered into the ceiling, blurs of color that her eyes shook to look at. She crushed the hilt in her hand.

*For her friends.*

The claws dug deeper into her neck.

*For the children.*

She could hear their invisible cries in her ears, telling her to get up.

*For the lives that were taken.*

The steel started to build between her fingers.

*For Lisa and Michael.*

*For Sally and Mitchell.*

*For Charlie.*

Its breath was hot against her nose, ruffled cries disguised as whispers held her ears tight.

*For the Lord.*

She whipped the blade, and the blue steel cut into the skin before it could block, before it could realize what it had done.

Blood tainted her white dress as the sword started to slip through half of its head. Its eyes widened with horror, the skin was prohibited from healing. Flesh tore and twisted, fell and moistened. A heart stopped beating; a brain halted its work. A human brain inside a monstrous skull, a human heart disappearing in the mutated body of something that used to be man.

Its horn stopped pulsing, and the top half of its head rolled onto the floor. Millie dropped the sword, the steel clattering in the mountains of stone she lay in. The heat that had radiated on her face ended, the glow that had created it had stopped working.

It was over, it was finally over.

They won, they could be free.

Yet, something tightened in her chest, a heart that she hadn't felt in a long time. A victory she didn't have the knowledge of gaining. She had a key for it, for a lock that she saw in front of her, and behind it, a glowing light that she loved dearly.

Though chips and broken pieces of the key were scattered around, the gold was nothing more than damaged and unusable. No longer a key, but lost hope. She wouldn't be able to open it on her own.

She walked to that light, that light behind the bars that held her away from it. She needed to know.

Millie dug deep into her mind, into a bottomless pit that had been covered long ago, memories that had been forced away, for the sake of this.

Millie forced the key into the lock, shoving it until the thing was shaped into what God needed it to be.

The lock of her memories opened, and the past was revealed.

Everything came back, everything she didn't know, she knew. The memories, the mission, the oath that had already been sworn way more far back then when she had promised it to God.

She had been sent here for one purpose. Protect the children that she had watched before the events of this lab, before it had been built. Her name wasn't even Millie, nor Experiment One.

The wings should have been a clear sign. She laughed at her own naivety; it was obvious, and she hadn't seen it. Tears were still on her cheeks above the stains that clung to her face, she wiped them away.

And now it was over, now she fulfilled the mission, and her friends were safe, and would finally…be happy.

She rose from the battle, a battle where she took victory, and held it close. Her body was dripping with blood of her own, and the monster that was slain before her. Her hands, her face, her legs, the injuries were too much; she couldn't take them any longer. Her power had drained her of life, and she wasn't getting either of them back. The blood covered her old scars, the scars she had gotten from the same monster long ago, about three years she believed. Millie stumbled, tripping over the leg of the monster that was now mutilated by her own hands, falling to the floor, unable to lift herself, from this madness.

She crawled over to the nearest wall, a wall that had trapped the cruel monster she had just fought. She rested her head against the cold stone, the stone that trapped children, traumatized children that she was supposed to protect, yet she had failed half of them, and she hoped they were safe up in the sky. A smile went across her face, a smile that was now full of her own blood, and the monsters.

The Lord works in mysterious ways.


The group rushed past the entry to the new way around. Charlie was the first to reach the corner and run past it but was frozen in absolute horror. Red splattered across the place. The disturbing sight of the monster lay before her, wanting to make her throw up in disgust, but her attention was thrown over to the victor, who was badly injured on the furthest wall. The shape of a pair of maroon wings formed over the gray floor, bloody, they could only see a hint of blue beneath the torn apart feathers.

"Millie!" Her voice was full of so many emotions without thought, just that this sight didn't look good, and the end result she imagined didn't look any better. Her hurry caused her to trip over the bloody claw of the monster, her head landing face first into the floor. Her eyes opened, only to scream in horror. Half the monster's head was gone, pierced by the blue tip of the sword Millie once wielded. The eyes that she thought she was going to see before her death, were ripped out and tossed to the side beside the body, she was offered a whole view of the flesh beneath its skin.

She squirmed away, reaching the almost dead body of Millie. But she saw her eyes. Those dark blue eyes were staring at her; she was alive still, but barely.

"Millie!" Charlie shouted again, her arms grabbing both sides of Millie's torso, an attempt to lift her, but it was nothing but a tremendous fail.

"Hey…" Millie mumbled, her voice was barely audible.

Charlie heard the footsteps of everyone behind her as she felt tears running down her face.

"We have to go! Before she—"

"Go," Millie interrupted her, the only reason being she didn't want the kids to hear the last word Lisa was about to speak, using some of the last bits of her remaining strength to lift her head.

"What?" both Charlie and Lisa said in unison, the rest said nothing.

"This is what you've all been fighting for, hasn't it?" Millie said, a smile appeared over her lips. "So, go. The exit is right behind you."

She saw the looks on their faces, the shock that controlled their dropped mouths; their eyes were full of words that they were unable to speak.

"We can't just leave you here!" Charlie shouted angrily, she was surprised at her own frustration, but she didn't care about that right now.

"It's okay, I did what I needed to do anyway," Millie claimed. The blood from her head covered half of her forehead like a blanket. Dark hot crimson, combined between hers and the monster's right behind her.

"What do you even mean by that? Millie please, you saved us. Let us save you..." Charlie cried, staring into the eyes of her friend.

"No, it's okay," Millie whispered, barely being able to talk. "Not–" A cough stopped her own words, blood sinking down her chin. "Not when I'm already done with what I was sent here for." The words were enough to make their cries go silent, the tormenting inner ones and the sobs that left their teeth.

"S–sent?" Charlie stuttered; that wasn't that much of an answer.

"My mission from God is complete," Millie explained. "I'm just leaving back to Him, I…guess."

Sally jumped through, landing right on Millie's lap, seeming unbothered by all red stains that massacred her white gown. Sally's arms were wrapped around Millie's body, tears flowing down her face, her teeth clenched, her eyes filling with tears of agony.

"Please don't go," the youngest girl pleaded, squeezing Millie tighter. Millie raised one hand, wrapping it around Sally's back. Sally knew blood was staining her hands, but the word of 'caring' was nonexistent.

"You'll be alright. All of you, will be okay. You don't need me anymore," Millie said, her smile, not leaving her face as her eyes slowly looked down at the anxious child hugging her. Tears rushed down her own face as well, her smile vanishing. "I'm sorry…I couldn't protect you fully, I couldn't stop it from hurting you. And I'm sorry I couldn't keep our promise, Charlie."

"Millie… please, we can get you help if you come with us," Lisa suggested, pointing to the exit standing behind them. She didn't care whether Millie was sent. She was her friend, human, or not.

"It's okay," Millie assured under her shaky breath. "I did my part, now you can do yours."

Lisa crouched down next to Charlie who shook rapidly.

"What's our part?" Lisa asked.

"Be free."

"Millie…" Charlie could only bare a whisper, the utter shock and grief inside her chained her words. She embraced Millie next to Sally; Charlie felt Lisa shuffle in next to her. Then Michael, then Mitchell. This was the one-time Michael has been silent, but she could hear the sobs choking him. The group embraced each other, embraced the being sent down to protect them. Their friend that decided their lives were more important than her own. The one that saved them all in the first place, yet they couldn't return the favor by saving her now. An oath, a sacrifice that they couldn't return. She couldn't return to the world with them.

"I'm so sorry, but this wasn't meant to last forever, no matter how much we want it to."

A spark emerged from Millie's arm, a spark of light that looked like a star. More followed afterwards, erasing half of Millie's limp arm. Her death wasn't stopping, but wasn't fast, as if her brothers and sisters were giving her time to say her goodbyes.

"Thank you for being my friends." The sparkles reached half of her head and most of her body, but that sweet old face remained smiling. The only sight she wanted to see before she died, was them.

"I'm so…" Lisa leaped forth, her arms scrambling through Millie's disappearing head; she touched nothing but blue sparkles. As if she could stop her friend's death, an angel's end as a human. She was so determined, yet she knew the outcome was buried beneath false faith and hope.

Soon Sally's legs hit the ground, as the angel vanished, and the stars that carried her soul traveled through the roof. Into the sky that looked over the earth they had spent three years on together.

The youngest burst into tears that she had been holding in for so long, lowering her head until it almost slammed into the ground. The weight of agony hit instead, cascading through her dripping hair like a waterfall. Lisa crouched in front of her, embracing her in an attempt to comfort her, while unsuccessfully holding in her own tears. Charlie felt the welled-up tears inside of her eyes; she didn't want to cry, but she let them go. Allowing them to fall onto the stone she could finally leave, finally escape. Everyone started crying, everyone screamed their tears that had built up since they took a step into this lab, this hell. And now, they were leaving for heaven, but...

She was gone, gone for the sake of their lives. It took such a long time, such a long time to let go of all the tears they had to relieve themselves of. If not for Charlie walking towards the exit with tears still running down her face, then the group would have been there forever, for eternity. The door swung open, and Charlie's eyes were blessed with the sight she had begged for her whole life in the lab.

The trees danced into Charlie's view as she exited the doorway, as she admired the beauty standing before her under all the grief that beat her stomach. The sun rose from the tall building behind her, glistening in the daylight she had dreamed of seeing for so long. New tears fell, tears of happiness, joy, under the sadness that washed over her. The outside world welcomed them into it once again.

Charlie heard the rest of the group leaving the building; she could even hear the smiles on their faces. A small forest lay ahead of them, but behind it was a town, a civilization, people. Cars, shops, roads, and birds, everything she had dreamt of and imagined was just ahead. Their happiness and joy were finally achieved. Their freedom, but at such a great loss, a cost they all grieved deeply, and would never forget that moment that would haunt them forever.

It was their dream, the one thing they hoped for. The world they wanted to see, the paradise they wanted to explore. Yet, it doesn't even look like that anymore when they stare closer, the Heaven they wanted. It isn't Heaven anymore.

Not without her.

# Chapter Nineteen

A Secret Guardian

Gabriel searched the place, the kitchen, the living room, Charlie's bedroom, their room, but he couldn't find her anywhere. He went back to the kitchen, only to find his wife, Elise, working on dinner.

"Hey, do you know where Charlie is?" he asked, scanning the place in case she was there, but she wasn't. It was just him and his wife.

"She's out in the backyard, just sitting there," Elise explained, pulling a jar out from the seasoning cabinet.

"She should come inside. It's been an hour."

"She hasn't seen it for this long, let her enjoy it," Elise ordered, "You do know that…right?" Her tone went serious at the last few words.

The back door of the house opened, a noise that made Charlie turn her head. Her father walked out, the brightness of the sun reflecting off his figure. She sat in the grass, feeling the cool feeling of it on her legs, letting her scars heal in the dearly craved sunlight.

"What are you up to?" he asked, plopping himself down by the girl.

"Looking at the sun." Charlie looked away for a little while to avoid the burning sensation in her eyes.

"Oh, interesting…what do you like about it?" She turned to him with a raised eyebrow.

"I don't know? It's the sun, it keeps us alive?" Charlie snickered, but he always enjoyed those. Her smile went into a frown swiftly; he followed when he saw the empty sorrow in her eyes.

"Sorry…" she muttered. "I just haven't seen it in a while."

"How are your friends?" Gabriel changed the topic, an awkward smile appearing in hopes to comfort her.

Charlie looked down at her phone, seeing the picture of all of them in the background. But she knew there was someone missing, someone she wished she could add, but that was impossible.

It all felt so confusing; she had so many questions. The twist still shocked her, yet it made her want to cry every time she thought about it. Charlie let out a loose breath. Her parents didn't know about it, nor did anyone else. The group had only explained that Experiment One had died killing the monster. The government hasn't talked about any more proposals with the continuation of the lab and its cruel experiments. Yet, she didn't know if she believed it.

"They're doing alright, Lisa and Michael are expecting a new sister."

"Really? When did this happen?"

"A couple days ago."

"That sounds exciting," Gabriel claimed, positioning himself to relax.

The breeze of the day was hard but also cool. It constantly tossed Charlie's hair back behind her, letting her feel the beauty of the outside world. She would never stop being grateful, she would never stop cherishing this world, even if she had lost someone so dear. She would never forget her or forget the trees. The sun, the moon, the stars; everything was now in her access, and she loved that so much.

She enjoyed the comfort of her bed, the comfort of the sheets. The blanket, everything felt so cozy, so comfortable, and so warm. Charlie lifted her hand to the ceiling, imagining it to be the stars over her head, the bright dots in the sky. The lights of the galaxy. Charlie closed her eyes, hoping to just teleport outside.

But she didn't, the comfort of the bed changed; it changed into something familiar. Charlie opened her eyes, only to see the familiar ceiling she hated to see for the three years of her life.

*No,* it felt so real, so—

Charlie raised her body, just to see the purple blanket of the bed, the empty room she slept in for so long. Her breath was so heavy, a fog that clouded her mind with sorrow.

Charlie exited the bed, feeling the rough wooden floors between her toes. The door to the room was wide open, letting in a chilling wind that flowed gently past her small body. It seemed to lead her out of the room, and she followed it. She had no idea why, everything screamed to hide, but...one small yet powerful thing beckoned her forward.

The hallway was dark, dark like the night before the escape. She saw the light of the main room, the safe room they all were glad to be out of, or what she thought. Charlie walked closer and closer to the light, a light that wasn't natural, in which she hated it just for that.

Charlie turned the corner, blinded by a light that was as bright as Lisa's power. Through that light, she saw something, someone, a small figure. Charlie squinted her eyes a little, only to be bitten by a white glow. She let her eyes adjust, blinking them rapidly until they could get used to it.

Her eyes were finally opened, and there she was, an old friend.

She stood from the couch she was sitting on, facing Charlie with a bright smile on her face.

"Hello Charlie. It's been a while; three weeks I believe?" Millie greeted casually, taking a step closer to Charlie's position. Charlie felt tears running down her face, and she wasn't going to stop them.

The room faded, revealing themselves to be in a bright void.

"M—Millie?"

Millie waved slowly with that same smile, her eyes closing cheerfully. She wasn't able to stop Charlie from flinging herself into her arms; tears were already forming in her eyes, stains appearing on Millie's white gown she still wore from the lab.

Those three weeks had been eternity for Charlie, like the deepest pits of hell without her friend.

"I'm so sorry," Charlie apologized for a reason Millie didn't know. "I'm so sorry for—"

"For what?" asked Millie. "Please don't apologize."

"But we left you, we left you to die—"

Millie squeezed her tighter; that was a clear sign to stop. Her cries were growing louder, her heart was beating rapidly in her chest.

"I blocked you off; that was my choice," said Millie. "Yet you still came back for me, didn't you?"

Charlie didn't shout out another response, she didn't have another word to speak besides sobs and her swallowed tears.

"I—I...still don't get it," muttered Charlie, her arms wrapped around Millie tighter. How long would they be here?

"Hm?"

"Why?"

Millie didn't answer for a moment; she seemed to be thinking about it.

"My memories of my past origin were erased," Millie explained. "I had no knowledge of who I was, to avoid sins of pride and arrogance. They're deadly and harmful, and we had bigger problems to deal with, didn't we?

"But I suppose my only hint was having the strong urge of loving the Lord so much," she chuckled, that sounded more like Millie than the fancy tone she had been using in this past 'dream,' though Charlie didn't understand if it was a dream or not.

"So...what about the lab? The government, do you know if they plan to..."

"There will be no more of it. They have nothing left, anyway."

"What?"

"Charlie…" Millie left the embrace, her smile vanishing into worried eyes, the same ones from the floor of the documents in the lab. "You believe it's your fault, don't you?"

Charlie stared in confusion with tears rolling down her cheeks, her lips unable to argue. "What?"

"Those voices in your head," Millie sighed. "You're telling yourself something awful and untrue."

Charlie's eyes widened, her body shaking, "How—"

"The Lord knows everything, dear."

Right, the secret her and everyone else had kept from the world, and yet she didn't realize it too. She rolled her eyes, a heavy weight thumping in her heart.

"You helped me once, I can help you again," Millie stepped closer. "I've talked to everyone else, but...do you want to talk about it?"

"I…" Charlie sniffed. "She—" Gosh, she didn't have words to talk with.

"You didn't speak up then, but you can now." Her hand landed on Charlie's shoulder. Charlie rubbed her tears away, her own arms squeezing her torso as hard as they ever did before.

"I should've told someone—" Charlie blurted. "I…was just too…"

"Afraid?" Millie finished for her. "Charlie, you had every reason to be, nobody would easily have a voice during a time like that. You were nine."

A sob left her throat, she was right. Charlie was aware; she knew Millie was correct, but yet, that haunting scream shouted the opposite of what her friend told her. Charlie ran back into Millie's arms. She didn't want to be done with this yet. Not ever, would she be ready to leave this.

"Your mother..." sounded Millie. "Forgives you. She loves you as she always has."

The same light as before began creeping into the room, Charlie didn't cover her eyes this time.

"See you there? In a couple fifty years?" It was so hard to say, yet the laugh wasn't. "Millie?" The safe room pulsed like a flickering light, as she awaited Millie's answer.

"See you there, Charlie. In a couple fifty years."

Her arms grazed the sheets of her new bed, and she awoke to a glittering moon in the night sky, slightly covered by the dark clouds. Blue flashed within their skin, as thunder roared into the night. Charlie sat up in her bed; the darkness of the room was nothing more than an inconvenience now, just like it would be for everyone else in everyday life. Her phone buzzed, and she reached for it on her nightstand. A hundred notifications, from Lisa and Michael, panicked, yet... relieved. Michael told her to watch the news. She checked Lisa's first, just to see a link to a live news broadcast.

Charlie clicked on it, and her heart thumped faster than it had ever done. Not out of fear, but joy.

The lab was on fire.

People cheered and roared, protestors that she had heard about who fought in their name. Who rallied against the government and asked for compensation for the victims. Because they ruined the children's lives. There was good in the world, a handful but still.

She jumped down from her bed, strolling to the window where she stared up at the stars. A yawn came from her throat. Millie was right; she recognized that now, despite how hard it was. She was watched over, by a lot of beings, and only one person.

Charlie noticed the dove sitting on a nearby branch after all it did, close to the glass. She watched as it soared to the moon, back to heaven, where she was conceived.

# About the Author

Madyson Evans started writing young at around 6th grade, recently winning a Scholastic silver key and honorable mention award, a Young Writers award, and a published poem from the American Library of Poetry. Growing up in Michigan, writing has become her voice. People have (probably) often questioned how dark the stories and tragedies she has written can get, that is yet to be answered.